Theodore W. Hunt

Caedmon's Exodus and Daniel

Theodore W. Hunt

Caedmon's Exodus and Daniel

Reprint of the original, first published in 1883.

1st Edition 2024 | ISBN: 978-3-38533-000-9

Verlag (Publisher): Outlook Verlag GmbH, Zeilweg 44, 60439 Frankfurt, Deutschland
Vertretungsberechtigt (Authorized to represent): E. Roepke, Zeilweg 44, 60439 Frankfurt, Deutschland
Druck (Print): Books on Demand GmbH, In de Tarpen 42, 22848 Norderstedt, Deutschland

CÆDMON'S

EXODUS AND DANIEL.

Edited from Grein.

BY

THEODORE W. HUNT, Ph. D.,

PROFESSOR OF RHETORIC AND ENGLISH LANGUAGE IN PRINCETON
COLLEGE.

BOSTON:

GINN, HEATH, AND COMPANY.

1883.

J. S. CUSHING & CO., PRINTERS, 115 HIGH STREET, BOSTON.

TABLE OF CONTENTS.

PREFACE.

ONE of the most urgent needs which the recent revival of interest in English Philology has brought to light is that of American editions of the best specimens of First English Prose and Poetry. So difficult of access and so expensive have the German, and even the English, editions been found, that the study of the oldest English has suffered not a little thereby. Nor is it altogether gratifying to the pride of an ingenuous American scholar to feel that he should be thus dependent upon foreign sources for the best results in this department. As far as the publication of Middle English Texts is concerned, the main work has been done, and naturally so, by native English scholars, such as Sweet, Earle, Skeat, and Morris, under the auspices of the Early English Text Society, and kindred agencies. As to the work of what has been called The Earliest English Text Society, most has been done by continental and English scholars. Such Danes and Germans as Rask, Bouterwek, and Grein, and such native Englishmen as Thorpe, Bosworth, Arnold, and Kemble, have been foremost in this arduous work. Up to a comparatively recent date, American scholarship had made no contributions to this subject. What was attempted was rather in the line of the elementary than in that of the more advanced and critical. To Professor March of Easton is due the awakening of a genuine interest in all that pertains to English speech, and more especially as to its first forms and uses. Since then, more or less of worthy work has been done at home by Corson, Carpenter, Cook, and Harrison. To Professor Harrison of Lexington special meed is due in beginning the editing of the best First English Poetry. His recent edition of Beówulf, from the text of Heyne, marks a new departure in the critical study of our mother tongue. It opens the way for a complete series of editions accessible in American forms, and at moderate cost. The present edition of Cædmon's Exodus and Daniel is in the way of contribution to this needed work, and is designed mainly for use in college classes. There is no part of our oldest poetry as good as Cædmon which is so difficult of access in this country, and of which there is more immediate need. The contemplated publication of the first part, Genesis, by Professor Price of Columbia College, and the edition of the second and third parts, now offered, will largely meet this need. It is gratifying to state that Professors March, Baskerville, and others will take part in the series proposed.

Of the various texts of Cædmon, there are four which any editor must have on his table: Junius, Thorpe, Bouterwek, and Grein. Of these, the last is by far the most valuable, and we shall adopt it as the authoritative text. We shall prefer to give Grein's text precisely as it stands in his *Poesie*, stating in our Critical Notes any important modifications suggested by the other editions referred to.

We deeply regret that Wülcker's Revision of Grein, so long promised, is not yet at hand. This will undoubtedly give us a text superior to any now extant; and, when it appears, may be used by the student in the way of helpful reference.

In addition to the text, with a brief outline of its separate sections, we shall give such notes as may seem to be needful, and include, also, a brief and yet sufficiently full glossary for the aid of the advanced student.

Much general introductory matter, such as the genuineness of the Paraphrase, and kindred topics, we must omit as properly belonging to the editor of Genesis, — Professor Price.

If the edition hereby offered aids a whit in the better study of our home speech, and deepens the interest already felt in a knowledge of its first forms, our final end will have been reached.

T. W. H.

Princeton College,
October, 1883.

GENERAL INTRODUCTION.

I. CÆDMON.

THIS "Father of English Song" appears in the earliest English history, and disappears from it, with but a fact here and there to fix his place and work. In the account of Cædmon given us by Alfred, in his translation of Bede's Ecclesiastical History, there are found a few incidents and statements which serve to make up his only biography. It is suggestive to note that this story in Bede reappears substantially in the Heliand, the old Saxon Paraphrase of the ninth century. It may further be noted that the fragment of song given us in this history is probably the most ancient piece of Saxon poetry extant.

From this we learn the following facts: That he was a native of Northumbria, near Whitby, and lived in the seventh century; that he was a convert from Paganism, and a member of the Abbey of Hilda; that he was English in heart and spiritual in life, singing in his native tongue, and always for holy ends; that he was a simple herdsman among his flocks, specially endowed in later life with the divine gift of poesy; that he wrote many poems; that he sang and prayed his life away in the love of God, and died in peaceful triumph about 680 A.D.

All we know of him is, that he was a pious monk, taught of God, full of song and Saxon spirit; and that out of the fulness of his heart, and for the common weal, he sang of Creation and of Christ.

II. THE PARAPHRASE.

1. Source of the Paraphrase.

This poem by Cædmon, as far as it is extant, is especially important to English scholars in that it marks the very beginning of Anglo-Saxon literature in the seventh century, its close being marked by the completion of the Chronicle in 1154.

As to its source, Bede and Alfred give us all that is to be given. In Thorpe's edition of Cædmon we may find a sufficiently accurate translation of this narrative. If this is not accessible, it may be found in any good history of the Anglo-Saxon, or in the Saxon text in March's Reader. The substance of the record in a few words is, that he was an untaught herdsman, ignorant of poetry; that, asleep among the cattle, he heard in his dream a voice bidding him sing; that, refusing, he was again commanded to sing the origin of things, and so began his song. At the request of the abbess, Hilda, he sang before all the learned, and turned into sweetest verse all that they taught him. Forsaking the worldly life, he joined the monks and devoted himself to the work of the minstrel. In this simple manner the origin of the Paraphrase and other poems has come down to later history.

2. Its Metrical Structure and Moral Character.

We find in Cædmon a good example of classic Saxon prose, a specimen of the language on the basis of which successful study may be conducted. As to the versification, it is that which all our First English Poetry has in common. We note the presence of alliteration, both of consonants and vowels, and the uniform division of the line into two sections (hemistichs), the cæsura falling between them. We note but few examples of final and perfect rhyme. The prevailing type of verse is the narrative with four feet in each poetic section. The long narrative verse is less frequent. As to accent or syllables determining the verse, we note the emphasis of the former, and this places our earliest poetry in harmony with our best modern poetry.

Centuries ago Bede stated the principle still in force, that "rhythm depends on the sound and modulation, and not on an artificial government of the syllables."

It may be added that parallelisms, which so mark the structure of Hebrew verse, are a conspicuous feature of the poetry in question, while there is found the same prevalence of metaphor, indirect statement, inversion, and abrupt transition that marks all our first poetry.

It is worthy of mention that Mr. Guest, in his English Rhythms, speaks of the special skill with which Cædmon manages his metres.

As to its moral character, the Paraphrase speaks for itself. It is a free poetic rendering of Holy Writ to foster piety in the hearts of the people.

It was the first attempt in English verse to popularize the Bible, and thus places its author in line with the authors of the Old Saxon Heliand, with Orm, Dante, Milton, and Klopstock, and with our own lamented Longfellow. The poem is spiritual throughout, and opens a question ill to solve, as to the presence in a converted pagan of such clear and high views of truth. It would be a study of no little interest to the student of theology to note the manner in which this "good monk of Whitby" paraphrases, in the seventh century, the Scriptural account of the fall of man and kindred doctrines.

There are reformers before the reformation, and Cædmon prepares the way for the great work of Wicliff and his successors.

3. Editions.

Of the old manuscript but one copy exists. Found in the seventeenth century by Usher, it came from him to Junius, who printed it at Amsterdam in 1655. The manuscript was given by Junius to the Bodleian Library at Oxford, where it is still preserved.

~~Its probable date is 731 A.D.~~ It is so defective that there must be much conjectural rendering, and much that after all study must remain hypothetical. To reduce these hypotheses has been the main object of Dr. Grein.

The manuscript is a small folio in parchment of 229 pages. Book I., made up of 212 of these pages, is written in a good hand, and is apparently of the tenth century, no religious Saxon manuscript being found earlier. The remaining 17 pages (Book II.) are imperfect in style and handwriting, and are probably later.

On the basis of this first text various editions have been given.

a. JUNIUS. As already stated, this was prepared at Amsterdam in 1655, a quarto edition. It is given in the ~~Old Saxon~~ without translation or comment, and often confuses the sense by the improper use of the metrical point. It is very valuable, however, in being the first authentic edition, and as opening the way for later and better work.

b. CONYBEARE (1826–7). This edition is found in the author's Illustrations of Anglo-Saxon Poetry, edited by his brother. It is but partial, and includes *Hymn of Cædmon*, *Speech of Satan* (Genesis), *The Deluge* (Exodus), *The Overthrow in the Red Sea* (Exodus).

It was by reason of this incomplete edition that Mr. Thorpe was induced to prepare another.

c. THORPE (1831–2). This ranks as the first Anglo-Saxon publication of the Society of Antiquaries in London. They assumed the entire expense of the edition, and enabled the editor to issue it in the most thorough and scholarly form. The text is given in Old Saxon, and is translated. By reason of the rareness of the work at this date, it is out of the reach of most students. The edition is based on the Bodleian manuscript, and is given with preface, notes, and a valuable verbal index. Whatever its defects of text and translation, it supplied an urgent need.

d. BOUTERWEK (1849). This edition is an exhaustive one. The introduction — literary and historical — is divided into eight sections. Then follows the text with critical notes, the translation into German prose with critical notes, and the Glossary, in Saxon and Latin, with explanations and suggestions. It closes with an Anglo-Latin verbal index, and an index of related Anglo-Saxon words.

e. GREIN (1857). This differs from Bouterwek and Thorpe in being untranslated, and more especially in constituting but a part of a large collection of Saxon verse (Grein's *Poesie*). Every English scholar must deeply regret the untimely death of Grein in that a corresponding collection of Saxon prose was planned and begun.

Prof. March is right when he says that "special students of Saxon must spend their days and nights with Grein."

This edition of poetry, including Cædmon, is accompanied with valuable notes, and a glossary which has no superior in modern scholarship. In Grein's first notice of the *Dichtungen der Angelsachsischen* (1857) he translates the poem on the basis of alliteration.

The revision of Grein promised by Wülcker will be awaited with great eagerness, as making a text already excellent still more correct.

f. ETTMÜLLER. In his *Scôpas and Bôceras* we find substantial parts of Genesis, and of Christ and Satan.

4. Contents of Paraphrase.

Book I., Genesis, 2935 lines; Exodus, 589 lines; Daniel, 765 lines. Book II., Christ and Satan, 733 lines. This second book is paraphrased from the New Testament, and is in every way inferior to the first. To these books some editors add *The Song of Azariah* and *The Song of the Three Children*. According to Bede, the Paraphrase is but a part of Cædmon's authorship. The full discussion of the authenticity of Cædmon, and a complete bibliography of the poem, is naturally left to the editor of Genesis, the first and largest poem of the collection.

5. Cædmon and Milton.

The history of opinion on this subject is full of interest. As favoring a close relationship, we note the names of Turner, Nicholson, Thorpe, Conybeare, Southey, and Taine, while such cautious writers as March and Morley hesitate not to give this theory the benefit of the doubt. Mr. Disraeli, in his Amenities of Literature, devotes an entire chapter to the subject, and takes strong ground against the theory of literary relation. The final settlement of this question is impossible. The facts are too few to warrant it. Each author had access to the Bible, and to biblical and mythical traditions, and drew from these common-sources. The coincidences are striking: each poem is in a sense a paraphrase of Scripture; each is an epic and on the same theme; each opens with the same scene, the fall of the angels, and proceeds in a somewhat similar manner. As to Satan's rebellion prior to the creation of man, and his consignment with the fallen angels to darkness and despair, they fully agree. The source whence they derived this tradition, Persian or Chaldean, must have been the same. Each poem points to the East as the place of origin, and many of the scenes and actors are the same. As to more specific resemblances, we may note the description of Satan and his fall; of hell and heaven; of Adam and Eve, and the speech of Satan to his rebel hosts. These coincidences, however, need not be regarded as proving identity or even actual imitation of plan. It is further to be noted that these similarities are found in Cædmon's Genesis only, the subject-matter of the other portions being outside of Milton's purpose. Even in Genesis there is a large part taken up with the history of Abraham, a topic, also, apart from Milton's aim. Moreover, the Paraphrase is based upon the Apocrypha as well as on the Canonical Scriptures. This collection of books is not endorsed by the Puritan poet. A word in reference to the historical relation of these two poets is here essential. The MS. of Junius (1655) may have been accessible to Milton. Morley writes: "Milton knew Junius [Cædmon's first editor], and was interested in his studies." The objection by Disraeli, that the MS. was too precious to be loaned by Junius, is unworthy of notice. To the graver objection, that the poet could not have read it in Saxon, it may be said, that Milton was a careful student of the earlier times. A few years before this he prepared a history of England up to the Norman Conquest in which he makes reference to the old authors. It is known that he was an Oriental scholar, and thoroughly versed in the Modern European Tongues, including some knowledge of the Low Dutch, so akin to the Saxon. Under the English government he was "secretary for foreign tongues." The argument here is, that it would not have been strange had such a linguist been able to read the Saxon of Junius. If not, the meaning could have been made known to him by Junius or Somner or others. By reason of the poet's blindness (1654) this was probably the case. Between the edition of Junius (1655) and the finishing of Paradise Lost (1661) there is a period of six years of possible reference to Cædmon. In fact, Milton's epic was not published till 1667, twelve years after Junius. The plausible theory, that a great poet cannot be indebted to his predecessors, is a mere hypothesis, and facts are against it. The England of Milton had something to learn from Bede and Alfred. We add the suggestion, that, in an epic upon the fall of man, the strong presumptive evidence is that Milton consulted any existing epic upon a similar theme. A translation by Bosanquet (1860) of the Miltonic portions of Cædmon into English Heroic Verse, fanciful as much of it is, is a valid proof of some substantial connection. He entitles his work, "The Paradise Lost of Cædmon." "Without doubt," says Wülcker, "the Genesis of Cædmon had made a deep impression upon the religious poet."

SPECIAL INTRODUCTION.

1. Theme and Plan of the Poems.

THE subject of Exodus is The Departure of Israel from Egypt, their Sojourn under Moses in the Wilderness, and their Passage through the Red Sea to the Land of Promise. Other portions of the Book of Exodus, as given in the Pentateuch, are omitted. The subject of Daniel is The Deliverance of the Three Hebrews from the Fiery Furnace. The poet takes the record, as in Exodus, from the Old Testament, giving a faithful paraphrase of the first five chapters of the Book of Daniel. For the sake of clearness the first of these poems may be divided, as in Grein, into eight sections, and the second into five. The topics of the respective sections will best be given in connection with the text.

2. State of the Text.

In common with other parts of Cædmon, and nearly all our earliest writers, the text is more or less unsatisfactory. Among the eight sections of Exodus there is one (VI.) that seems to have been bodily interpolated, while in the third section of Daniel there is a very loose paraphrase of Azarias as given in The Codex Exoniensis, or Exeter Book. The addition of single words and lines is very common, as also their omission. In the best editions there are several textual gaps which the editors do not pretend to supply. In many other places no one can be dogmatic as to the rendering. Despite these facts, however, the substantial correctness and unity of Exodus and Daniel are preserved.

3. Literary Character.

The cast of the poems is lyrical as well as epic. Moses and Pharaoh, Daniel, Nebuchadnezzar, Belshazzar, and the Hebrew children are the prominent figures, while the praises of Jehovah and his servants are sung in fervid strain. They afford one of the best examples in our literature of the combination of the narrative style proper to the epic, with the freer descriptive style of impassioned verse. Where they lack in smoothness of historical order they abound in imaginative sketching of persons and scenes. Some of the descriptions are as bold and vivid as those of Beôwulf, "the Saxon Homer." In this respect they surpass Genesis, and have always been regarded as poems of rare interest, especially characteristic of early Teutonic literature. They are in the department of the sacred epic what Beôwulf is in the historico-mythical epic, marked by the old Gothic dash and daring.

Their influence is stimulating. They stir the blood. They are a bold testimony by a converted Pagan to the power of Jehovah on behalf of his oppressed people. We think, as we read them, of the most stirring battle songs of the Bible, and of secular letters. They have the same martial spirit. It is for reasons such as these that we have deemed it wise to place these poems in reach of American students. It is hoped that they will aid in the critical study of First English, and infuse into the modern Teuton something of that Saxon vigor to which he has rightful heirship.

CÆDMON'S

EXODUS AND DANIEL.

EXODUS.

I.

Hwæt! we feor and néah gefrigen habbað
ofer middangeard Moyses dómas
wræclíco word-riht wera cnéorissum,
in uproder éádigra gehwam
5 æfter bealusíðe bóte lífes,
lifgendra gehwam langsumne ræd
hæleðum secgan ; gehýre se þe wille!
Þone on wéstenne weroda drihten
sóðfæst cyning mid his sylfes miht
10 gewyrðode and him wundra fela
éce alwalda in æht forgeaf.
He wæs léof gode, léoda aldor,
horsc and hreðergléaw herges wísa,
freom folctoga. Faraones cyn
15 godes andsacan gyrdwíte band,
þær him gesealde sigora waldend
módgum magoræswan his mága feorh, .
onwist éðles Abrahames sunum.

NOTE. — The student is referred to the Notes for all the important differences between the text of Grein and that of other editors.

Héah wæs þæt handléan and him hold fréa
20 gesealde wæpna geweald wið wráðra gryre :
ofercom mid þý campe cneómága fela,
féonda folcriht.   Þá wæs forma sið,
þæt hine weroda god wordum nægde,
þær he him gesægde sóðwundra fela,
25 hú þás woruld worhte witig drihten,
eorðan ymbhwyrft and uprodor
gesette sigeríce, and his sylfes naman,
þone yldo bearn ær ne cúðon,
fród fædera cyn, þéah hie fela wiston.
30 Hæfde he þá geswíðed sóðum cræftum
and gewurðodne werodes aldor
Faraones féond on forðwegas,
þá wæs iu-gére ealdum wítum
déaðe gedrenced drihtfolca mæst :
35 hordwearda hryre héaf wæs geniwad,
swæfon seledréamas since berofene ;
hæfde mánsceaðan æt middere niht
frécne gefylled, frumbearna fela,
ábrocene burhweardas : bana wíde scráð,
40 láð léodhata.   Land drysmyde
déadra hræwum : dugoð forð gewát,
wóp wæs wíde, worulddréama lyt !
wæron hleahtorsmiðum handa belocene,
ályfed ládsíð léode grétan,
45 folc férende : féond wæs beréafod,
hergas on helle.   Heofon-þíder becom,
druron déofolgyld.   Dæg wæs mære
ofer middangeard, þá seó mengeo fór,
swá þæs fæsten dréath fela missera
50 caldwérige Egypta folc,
þæs þe hie wíde-ferð wyrnan þohton
Moyses mágum, gif hie metod léte,
onlangne lust léofes síðes.

Fyrd wæs gefýsed, from se þe lædde
55 mödig magoræswa mægburh heora.
Oferför he mid þý folcê fæstena worn
land and lêðdweard lâðra manna,
enge ânpaðas, uncûð gelâd,
ôð þæt hie on Gûðmyrce gearwe bæron;
60 wæron land heora lyfthelmê beþeaht
mearchofu môrheald: Moyses ofer þâ
fela meoringa fyrde gelædde.
Hêht þâ ymb twâ niht tîrfæstne hæleð,
siððan hie fêðndum ôðfaren hæfdon,
65 ymbwîcigean werodes bearhtmê
mid ælfere Æthanes byrig
mægnes mæstê mearclondum on.

II.

The protection of the people by Jehovah. — The third encampment. — The pillar of cloud and of fire. — The joyful
breaking of camp. — The heavenly beacon. — The approach
to the sea. — Encampment at the Red Sea.

Nearwe genêðdon on norðwegas,
wiston him be sûðan Sigelwara land,
70 forbærned burhhleoðu, brûne lêðde
hâtum heofoncolum. Þær hâlig god
wið færbryne folc gescylde,
bælcê oferbrædde byrnendne heofon,
hâlgan nettê hâtwendne lyft.
, 75 Hæfde wederwolcen wîdum fæðmum
eorðan and uprodor efne gedæled,
lædde lêðdwerod: ligfýr âdranc
hât heofontorht. Hæleð wafedon,
drihta gedrýmost. Dægsccaldes hlêð

80 wand ofer wolcnum : hæfde witig god
    sunnan siôfæt segle ofertolden,
    swâ þâ mæst-râpas men ne cûðon
    ne þâ seglrôde geséôn meahton
    corðbûende eallê cræftê,
85 hû âfæstnod wæs feldhûsa mæst.
    Siððan he mid wuldre geweorðode
    péôden holde, þâ wæs þridda wîc
    folce tô frôfre : fyrd eall geseah,
    hû þær hlifedon hâlige seglas,
90 lyftwundor léôht ; léôde ongéton,
    dugoð Israhéla, þæt þær drihten cwom,
    weroda drihten, wîcsteal metan.
    Him beforan fôran fŷr and wolcen
    in beorht-rodor, béâmas twegen,
95 þâra æghwæðer efn-gedælde
    héâhþegnunga hâliges gâstes
    déôrmôdra sîð dagum and nihtum.
    þâ ic on morgen gefrægn môdes rôfan
    hebban herebŷman hlûdan stefnum,
100 wuldres wôman.   Werod eall ârâs,
    môdigra mægen, swâ him Moyses bebéâd
    mære magoræswa metodes folce,
    fûs fyrdgetrum : forð gesâwon
    lîfes lâtþéôw lîftweg metan.
105 Segl stôc wéôld, sæ-men æfter
    fôron flôdwegê ; folc wæs on sâlum,
    hlûd herges cyrm.   Heofonbéâcen âstâh
    æfena gehwam : ôðer wundor
    syllîc æfter sunnan setlrâde behéôld
110 ofer léôdwerum lîgê scînan,
    byrnende béâm.   Blâce stôdon
    ofer scéôtendum scîre léôman,
    scinon scyldhréôðan, sceado swiðredon :
    neowle nihtscuwan neah ne mihton

115　heolstor âhŷdan.　Heofoncandel bearn :
　　niwe nihtweard nŷde sceolde
　　wîcian ofer weredum, þŷ læs him wêstengryrê
　　hâr hæð holmegum wedrum
　　ô fêrclammê ferhð getwæfde.
120　Hæfde foregenga fŷrene loccas,
　　blâce beámas, bæl-egsan hweôp
　　þam hereþreâte, hâtan lîgê,
　　þæt he on wêstenne werod forbærnde,
　　nymðe hie môdhwate Moyses hŷrde.
125　Sceân scîr werod, scyldas lixton ;
　　gesâwon randwîgan rihtre stræte
　　segn ofer sweôtum, ôð þæt sæfæsten
　　landes æt ende leôdmægne forstôd,
　　fûs on forðweg.　Fyrdwîc ârâs,
130　wyrpton hie wêrige ; wiste genægdon
　　môdige meteþegnas hyra mægen bêtan.
　　Bræddon æfter beorgum, siððan bŷme sang,
　　flotan feldhûsum : þâ wæs feôrðe wîc
　　randwîgena ræst be þam reâdan sæ.

　　　　　　　　　　III.

Fear of Pharaoh in pursuit. — Sins of Egypt. — Pursuit by
Pharaoh and his host. — Increasing terror of the people. —
Preparation for battle.

135　　Þær on fyrd hyra færspell becwom,
　　ôht inlende : egsan stôdan,
　　wælgryre weroda.　Wræcmon gebâd
　　lâðne lâstweard, se þe him lange ær
　　eðelleâsum ôht-nied gescrâf,
140　weân wîtum fæst : wære ne gŷmdon,
　　þeâh þe se yldra cyning ær ge[tiðode],

þâ [he] wearð yrfeweard in-gefolca
manna æfter mâðmum, þæt he swâ miceles geþâh :
ealles þæs forgêton, siððan grame wurdon
145 Egypta cyn ymb andwîg,
þâ heo his mægwinum morðor fremedon,
wrôht berênodon, wære fræton.
Wæron heaðowylmas heortan getenge,
mihtmôd wera mânum trêowum :
150 woldon hie þæt feorhlêan fâcne gyldan,
þætte he þæt dægweorc drêorê gebohte,
Moyses lêode, þær him mihtig god
on þam spildstôc spêde forgêfe.
þâ him eorla môd ortrŷwe wearð,
155 siððan hie gesâwon of sûðwegum
fyrd Faraones forð ongangan,
oferholt wegan, êored lixan,
þûfas þunian, þêod mearc tredan :
gâras trymedon, gûð hwearfode,
160 blicon bordhrêoðan, bŷman sungon.
On hwæl hrêopon herefugolas
hilde grædige ; [hræfen gôl]
dêawigfeðere ofer driht-nêum,
wonn wælcêasega. Wulfas sungon
165 atol æfenlêoð ætes on wênan,
carlêasan dêor, cwyld-rôf bêodan
on lâðra lâst lêodmægnes fyll,
hrêopon mearcweardas middum nihtum :
flêah fæge gâst, folc wæs genæged.
170 Hwîlum of þam werode wlance þegnas
mæton mîlpaðas meara bôgum.
Him þær sigecyning wið þone segn foran
manna þengel mearcþrêatê râd ;
gûðweard gumena grîmhelm gespêon
175 ciuing ciuberge (cumbol lixton)
wîges on wênum, wælhlencan sceôc,

hêht his herecíste healdan georne
fæst fyrdgetrum.　Fêond onségon
láðum éâgum landmanna cyme.
180 Ymb hine wægon wígend unforhte,
　hâre heorowulfas hilde grêtton
　þurstige þræcwíges þêoden holde.
　Hæfde.him âlesen lêoda dugeðe
　tîr-éâdigra twâ þûsendo,
185 þæt wæron cyningas and cnêowmâgas,
　on þæt éâde riht æðelum dêore ;
　forþon ânra gehwilc ût âlædde
　wæpnedcynnes wígan æghwilcne,
　þâra þe he on þam fyrste findan mihte.
190 Wæron inge men ealle ætgædere
　cyningas on corðre : cûðost gebêâd
　horn on hêâpe, tô hwæs hægstealdmen
　gûðþrêât gumena gearwe bæron.
　Swâ þær eorp werod êcan læddon
195 láð æfter láðum lêodmægnes worn
　þûsendmælum, þider wæron fûse :
　hæfdon hie gemynted tô þam mægenhêâpum
　tô þam ærdæge Israhêla cynn
　billum âbrêotan on hyra brôðorgyld.
200 Forþon wæs on wícum wôp up âhafen,
　atol æfenlêoð.　Egesan stôdon,
　weredon wælnet, þâ se wôma cwom,
　flugon frêcne spel : fêond wæs anmôd,
　werud wæs wígblâc, ôð þæt wlance forscêâf
205 mihtig engel, se þâ menigeo behêold,
　þæt þær gelâðe mid him leng ne mihton
　geséon tôsomne : slð wæs gedæled.

IV.

*Renewed fear and further preparation. — Description of the
host under Moses.*

Hæfde nŷdfara nihtlangne fyrst,   .
pêah pe him on hêâlfa gehwam hettend seomedon,
210 mægen oððe merestrêâm : nâhton mâran hwyrft,
wæron orwênan ôôclrihtes,
sæton æfter beorgum in blâcum rêâfum
wêân on wênum.   Wæccende bâd
call sêô sibgedriht somod ætgædere
215 mâran mægenes, ôð Moyses bebêâd
eorlas on uhttîd ærnum bêmum
folc somnigean, frecan̩ ârîsan,
habban heora hlencan, hycgan on ellen,
beran beorht searo, bêâcnum cîgean
220 swêôt sande nêâr : snelle gemundon
weardas wîglêôð.   Werod wæs gefŷsed :
brudon ofer beorgum (bŷman gehŷrdon)
flotan feldhûsum.   Fyrd wæs on ôfste,
siððan hie getealdon wið pam têônhete
225 on pam forðherge fêðan twelfe
môdê rôfa ; mægen wæs onhrêred.
Wæs on ânra gehwam æðeles cynnes
âlesen under lindum lêôda duguðe
on folcgetæl fîftig cista ;
230 hæfde cista gehwilc cûðes werodes
gârberendra gûðfremmendra
tyn-hund geteled tîr-êâdigra.
Pæt wæs wîglîc werod : wâcc ne grêtton
in pæt rincgetæl ræswan herges,
235 pâ pe for gêôguðe gyt ne mihton
under bordhrêôðan brêôstnct wera

wið flâne féond folmum werigean
ne him bealu benne gebiden hæfdon
ofer linde lærig ; lícwunde swor,
240 gylpplegan gâres.　Gamele ne môston
hâre heaðorincas hilde onþéon,
gif him môdhéapum mægen swiðrade :
ac hie be wæstmum wíg curon,
hû in léodscipe læstan wolde
245 môd mid âran, éac þan mægnes cræft
[gegân mihte] gârbéames feng.
þâ wæs handrôfra here ætgædere
fûs forðwegas.　Fana up-râd,
béama beorhtest : bidon ealle þâ gen,
250 hwonne síðboda sæstréamum néah
léoht ofer lindum lyft-edoras bræc.

V.

The harangue of Moses to the host. — Charge to be courageous.
— Assurance of God's help. — Dividing of the waters by
Moses. — The rising of the host. — Entrance on the sea
path. — The march over the sea by tribes. — Description of
tribes. — Judah, Reuben, and Simeon.

Ahléop þâ for hæleðum hildecalla,
beald béot-hâta, bord up âhôf,
hêht þâ folctogan fyrde gestillan,
255 þenden môdiges meðel monige gehŷrdon.
Wolde reordigean ríces hyrde
ofer hereciste hâlgan stefne ;
werodes wísa wurðmyndum spræc :
Ne béoð ge þŷ forhtran, þéah þe Faraon brohte
260 sweordwígendra síde hergas,
eorla unrîm !　Him eallum wile

mihtig drihten þurh míne hand
tó dæge þissum dædléan gyfan,
þæt hie lifigende leng ne móton
265 ægnian mid yrmðum Israhéla cyn.
Ne willað éow ondrædan déáde féðan
fæge ferhðlocan ! fyrst is æt ende
lænes lífes. Eow is lár godes
ábroden of bréóstum : ic on beteran ræd,
270 þæt ge gewurðien wuldres aldor
and éow líffréán lissa bidde,
sigora gesynto, þær ge stíðien !
Þis is se écea Abrahames god,
frumsceafta fréá, se þás fyrd wereð
275 módig and mægenróf mid þære miclan hand.
Hóf þá for hergum hlúde stefne
lifigendra léód, þá he tó léódum spræc :
Hwæt ! ge nu éágum tó on lóciað,
folca léófost, færwundra sum.
280 hú ic sylfa slóh and þéós swíðre hand
gréné táné gársecges déóp :
ýð up færeð, ófstum wyrceð
wæter and wealfæsten. Wegas syndon drýge,
haswe herestræta, holm gerýmed,
285 ealde staðolas, þá ic ær ne gefrægn
ofer middangeard men geféran,
fámge feldas, þá forð heonon
iu éce ýðe þeahton,
sælde sægrundas : súðwind fornam
290 bæðweges blæst, brim is áréáfod,
sand sæcir spáw. Ic wát sóð gere,
þæt éow mihtig god miltse gecýðde,
eorlas, ær gláde ! ófest is sélost,
þæt ge of féónda fæðme weorðen,
295 nu se ágend up árærde
réáde stréámas in randgebeorh :

syndon þâ foreweallas fægre gestêpte
wrætlîcu wægfaru ôð wolcna hrôf.
Æfter þâm wordum werod eall ârâs,
300 môdigra mægen : mere stille bâd.
Hôfon herecyste hwîte linde,
segnas on sande. Sæweall âstâh,
uplang gestôd wið Israhêlum
ândægne fyrst ; wæs sêo eorla gedriht
305 ânes môdes : [fða weall]
fæstum fæðmum freoðowære hêold.
Nalles higê gehyrdon hâliges lâre,
s3iððan lêofes lêoð læste neâr
swêg swiðrode and sanges bland.
310 Þâ þæt fêorðe cyn fyrmest êode,
wôd on wægstrêâm, wîgan on heâpe,
ofer grênne grund : Judisc fêða
ân ou-orette uncûð gelâð
for his mægwinum, swâ him mihtig god
315 þæs dægweorces dêop lêan forgeald,
siððan him gesælde sigorworca hrêð,
þæt he ealdordôm âgan sceolde
ofer cynerîcu, cnêowmâga blæd.
Hæfdon him tô segne, þâ hie on sund stigon,
320 ofer bordhrêðan beâcen âræred
in þam gârheâpe gyldenne leon,
drihtfolca mæst dêora cênost :
be þam herewîsan hŷnðo ne woldon
be him lifigendum lange þolian,
325 þonne hie tô gûðe gârwudu rærdon,
þêoda ænigre. Þracu wæs on ôre,
heard handplega, hægsteald môdige
wæpna wælslihtes, wîgend unforhte,
bilswaðu blôdige, beadumægnes ræs,
330 grîmhelma gegrind, þær Judas fôr.
Æfter þære fyrde flota môdgade,

Rubenes sunu : randas bæron
sæwícinge ofer sealtne mersc,
mán menio, micel án-getrum
- 335 éôðle unforht.   Hê his ealdordôm
synnum áswefede, þæt hê síðor fôr
on léôfes lást : him on léôdsceare
frumbearnes riht fréôbrôðor ôðþah,
éâd and æðelo ; hê wæs earu swá þéâh.
340 þær [forð] æfter him folca þryðum
sunu Simeones swéôtum cômon,
þridde þéôdmægen : þúfas wundon
ofer gárfare, gúðcyst onþrang
déâwig sceaftum.   Dægwôma beewom
345 ofer gársecges [begong], godes béâcna sum,
morgen mære-torht.   Mægen forð gewát,
þá þær folcmægen fôr æfter ôðrum :
ísernhergum án wísode
mægenþrymmum mæst, þý hê mære wearð.
350 [Fôr] on forðwegas folc æfter wolcnum,
cynn æfter cynne : cúðe æghwilc
mægburga riht, swá hím Moyses béâd,
eorla æðelo.   Him wæs án fæder :
léôf léôdfruma landriht geþah
355 frôd on ferhðe, fréômágum léôf,
eende cnéôwsibbe cénra manna,
héâhfædera sum hálige þéôde,
Israêla cyn, onriht gôdes,
swá þæt orþancum ealde reccað,
360 þá þe mægburge mæst gefrunon,
frumcyn feora, fæderæðelo gehwæs.

VI.

Noah and his sons in the ark. — The contents of the ark. —
Abraham, the people's guide and lord. — David and Solo-
mon. — Abraham and Isaac on the way to the mount. —
Preparations for the sacrifice. — Arrest by the angel. —
Jehovah's promise as to Abraham's seed.

　　　Niwe flôdas Noe oferlâð
　　　þrymfæst féðden mid his þrîm sunum,
　　　þone déopestan drencflôda
365　þara þe gewurde on woruldrîce.
　　　Hæfde him on hreðre hâlige tréowa:
　　　forþon hê gelædde ofer lagustréamas
　　　mâðmhorda mæst mîné gefrægé:
　　　on feorhgebeorh folden hæfde
370　eallum eorðcynne ege-lâfe
　　　frumenéow gehwæs, fæder and môder
　　　tuddor-téondra geteled rîmé
　　　mismicelra, þonne men çunnon,
　　　snottor sæleoda; éac þon sæda gehwilc
375　on bearm scipes beornas feredon,
　　　þâra þe under heofonum hæleð bryttigað.
　　　Swâ þæt wîse men wordum secgað,
　　　þæt from Noe nigoða wære
　　　fæder Abrahames on folctale:
380　þæt is se Abraham, se him engla god
　　　naman niwan âsceôp, éac þon néah and feor
　　　hâlige héapas in gehyld bebéad,
　　　werþéoda geweald. Hê on wræce lifde.
　　　Siððan hê gelædde léofost feora
385　hâliges hæsum: héahlond stigon
　　　sibgemâgas on Seone beorg;
　　　wære hie þær fundon, wuldor gesâwon,

hâlige hêahtrêowe, swâ hæleð gefrunon,
þær eft se snottra sunu Dauides
390 wuldorfæst cyning witgan lârum
getimbrede tempel gode,   •
alh hâlignę, corðcyninga
se wîsesta on woruldrîce
hêahst and hâligost hæleðum gefrægost
395 mæst and mærost, þâra þe manna bearn
fira æfter foldan folmum geworhte.
Tô þam meðelstede magan gelædde
Abraham Isaac ; âdfŷr onbran :
fyrst ferhðbana nô þŷ fægra wæs !
400 Wolde þone lâstweard lîge gesyllan
in bælblŷse beorna sêlost
his swæsne sunu tô sigetibre,
ângan ofer eorðan yrfelâfe,
feores frôfre.   þâ hê swâ forð gebâd
405 lêodum tô lâre langsumne liht :
hê þæt gecŷðde, þâ hê þone cniht genam
fæste mid folmum, folccûð getêag
ealde lâfe (ecg grymetode),
þæt hê him lîfdagas lêofran ne wisse,
410 þonne hê hŷrde heofoncyninge.
Up âræmde se eorl, wolde slean eaforan sînne,
unweaxenne ecgum rêðdan,
magan mid mêcê, gif hine metod lête :
ne wolde him beorht fæder bearn ætniman
415 hâlig tiber, ac mid handa bifêng.
þâ him stŷran cwom stefn of heofonum,
wuldres blêðður, word æfter spræc : •
Ne sleh þû, Abraham, þîn âgen bearn
sunu mid sweordê ! sôð is gecŷðed,
420 nu þîn cunnode cyning alwihta,
þæt þu wið waldend wære hêolde,
fæste trêowe : sêð þe freoðo sceal

in lîfdagum lengest weorðan
âwa tô ealdre unswîciendo !
425 hû þearf mannes sunu mâran trêowe?
    Ne behwylfan mæg heofon and eorðe
    his wuldres word wîddra and sîddra
    þonne befæðman mæge foldan scêatas,
    eorðan ymbhwyrft and uprodor,
430 gârsecges gin and þêos gêomre lyft.
    Hê âð swereð, engla þêoden,
    wyrda waldend and werela god,
    sôðfæst sigora [weard], þurh his sylfes lîf,
    þæt þînes cynnes and cnêowmâga
435 randwiggendra rîm ne cunnon
    ylde ofer eorðan eallê cræftê
    tô gesecgenne sôðum wordum,
    nymðe hwylc þæs snottor in sefan weorðe,
    þæt hê âna mæge ealle gerîman
440 stânas on eorðan, steorran on heofonum,
    sæbeorga sand, sealte ŷða :
    ac hie gesittað be sæm twêonum
    Oð Egypte in-geþêode
    land Cananêa, lêode þîne,
445 frêobearn fæder, folca sêlost.

VII.

Pharaoh's host is overwhelmed in the sea.

    Folc wæs âfæred : flôdegsa becwom
    gâstas gêomre, geofon dêðê hwêop.
    Waêron beorhhliðu blôdê bestêmed,
    holm heolfrê spâw, hrêam wæs on ŷðum,
450 wæter wæpna ful, wælmist âstâh.
    Waêron Egypte eft oncyrde,

flugon forhtigende, fær ongêton,
woldon hereblêðc hâmas findan :
gylp wearð gnornra!   Him on-gen gehnâp
455 atol ȝða gewealc : ne þær ænig becwom
herges tô hâme, ac hie hindan belêâc
wyrd mid wæge.   Þær ær wegas lâgon,
⸜mere môdgode, mægen wæs âdrenced.
Strêâmas stôdon ; storm up gewât
460 hêâh tô heofonum, herewôpa mæst ;
lâðe cyrmdon ; lyft up geswearc :
fægum stæfnum flôd blôd gewôd.
Randbyrig waêron rofene, rodor swipode
meredêâða mæst ; môdige swulton
465 cyningas on corðre, cyrr swiðrode
wæges æt ende.   Wîgbord scinon.
Hêâh ofer hælcðum holmweall âstâh,
merestrêâm môdig : mægen wæs on cwealme
fæste gefeterod, forðganges nêp
470 searwum âsæled.   Sand bâsnode
on witodre fyrde, hwonne waðema strêâm
sincalda sæ sealtum ȝðum
æflâstum gewuna êce staðulas
nacud nȳdboda nêðsan côme,
475 fâh fêðe-gâst, se þe fêôndum gencôp.
Wæs sêô hæwene lyft heolfrê geblanden ;
brim berstende blôdegsan hwêôp,
sæmanna stô, ôðþæt sôð metod
þurh Moyses hand môdge rȳmde :
480 wîde wæôde, wælfæðmum swêôp,
flôd fâmgode, fæge crungon,
laguland gefêôl, lyft wæs onhrêred,
wicon weallfæsten, wægas burston,
multon meretoras, þâ se mihtiga slôh
485 mid hâlige hand heofonrîces weard
werbêâmas, wlance þêôde.

Ne mihton forhabban helpendra paŏ,
merestreámes mód, ac hé manegum gesceód
gyllendé gryré : gársecg wédde,
490 up átéah, on sléap ; egesan stódon,
wéŏllon wælbenna. Witród gesceól
héah of heofonum, handweorc godes.
Fámigbósma flódwearde slóh
unhléŏwan wæg aldé mécé,
495 þæt þý déaŏdrepé drihte swæfon,
synfullra swéŏt, sáwlum lunnon
fæste befarene, flódblác here,
siŏŏan hie onhugon brún yppinge,
módwæga mæst. Mægen eall gedréás,
500 þá hé gedrencte dugoŏ Egypta,
Faraon mid his folcum : hé onfond hraŏe,
siŏŏan [grund] gestáh, godes andsaca,
þæt þær mihtigra mereflódes weard
wolde heorofæŏmum hilde gesceádan
505 yrre and egesfull.   Egyptum wearŏ
þæs dægweorces déóp léan gesceod :
forþam þæs heriges hám eft ne com
ealles ungrundes ænig tó láfe,
þætte síŏ heora secgan móste,
510 bodigean æfter burgum bealospélla mæst,
hordwearda hryre hælcŏa cwénum,
ac þá mægenþreátas meredéáŏ geswealh,
[spilde] spelbodan, se þe spéd áhte,
ágéat gylp wera : hie wiŏ god wunnon !

VIII.

Words of Moses to Israel on the farther shore. — God's power and covenant faithfulness. — The joy of the people upon their deliverance. — Division of spoil.

515 Þanon Israhelum éce rædas
     on merehwearfe Moyses sægde
     héahþungen wer hálige spræce,
     déop ærende : dægweorc nemnað.
     Swá gyt werþéode on gewritum findað
520 dóma gehwilcne, þára þe him drihten bebéad
     on þam stðfate sóðum wordum.
     Gif onlúcan wile lífes wealhstód
     beorht in bréostum bánhúses weard
     ginfæst god gástes cægum,
525 rún bið gerecenod, ræd forð gæð :
     hafað wislícu word on fæðme,
     wile méagollíce módum tæcan,
     þæt wé gésine ne sýn godes þéodscipes,
     meotodes miltsa.   Hé ús má onlýhð,
530 nú ús bóceras beteran secgað,
     lengran lýft wynna : þis is læne dréam
     wommum áwyrged, wreccum álýfed,
     earmra anbíd : éðellðáse
     þysne gystsele gihðum healdað,
535 murnað on móde, mánhús witon
     fæst under foldan, þær bið fýr and wyrm,
     open éce scræf yfela gehwylces.
     Swá nú reguþéofas ríce dælað
     yldo oððe ær-déað, eft-wyrd cymð
540 mægenþrymma mæst ofer middangeard,
     dæg dædum fáh : drihten sylfa
     on þam meðelstede manegum démeð.

Þonne hê sôðfæstra sâwla lædeð
êadige gæstas on uprodor,
545 þær [is] lêoht and lîf, êac þon lissa blæd:
dugoð on drêame drihten hêrigað
weroda wuldorcyning tô wîdan feore.
Swâ reordode ræda gemyndig
manna mildost mihtum swîðed
550 hlûdan stefne ; here stille bâd
witodes willan, wundor ongêton,
môdiges mûðhæl ; hê tô mænegum spræc :
Micel is þêos menigeo, mægenwîsa trum,
fullêsta mæst, se þâs fare lædeð l
555 hafað ûs on Cananêa cyn gelŷfed
burh and bêagas, brâde rîce :
wile nû gelæstan, þæt hê lange gehêt
mid âðsware, engla drihten,
in fyrndagum fæderyn-cynne,
560 gif ge gehealdað hâlige lâre,
þæt ge fêonda gehwone forð ofergangað,
gesittað sigerîce be sæm twêonum
bêorselas beorna : bið êower blæd micel l
After þâm wordum werod wæs on sâlum,
565 sungon sigebŷman, segnas stôdon
on fægerne swêg. Folc wæs on lande :
hæfde wuldres bêam werud gelæded
hâlige hêapas on hild godes.
Lîfê gefêgon, þâ hie ôðlæded hæfdon
570 feorh of fêonda dôme, þêah þe hie hit frêcne genêðdon
weras under wætera hrôfas. Gesâwon hie þær
        weallas standan ;
ealle him brimu blôdige þûhton, þurh þâ heora beado-
        searo wægon.
Hrêðdon hildespellê, siððan hie þam [herge] wiðfôron,
hôfon hereþrêatas hlûde stefne,
575 for þam dædweorce drihten hêredon :

weras wuldres sang, wîf on ôðrum,
folcswêôta mæst fyrdlêôð gôlon
aclum stefnum eallwundra fela.
Þâ wæs êôfynde Afrisc mêôwle
580 on geofones staðe goldê geweorðod :
hand âhôfon hâlswurðunge,
blîðe waêron, bôte gesâwon,
hêddon hererêâfes (hæft wæs onsæled),
ongunnon sælâfe segnum dælan
585 on fôlâfe, ealde mâðmas,
rêâf and randas : heom on riht sceode
gold and godweb, Josephes gestrêôn
wera wuldorgesteald. Werigend lâgon
on dêâðstede, drihtfolca mæst.

DANIEL.

I.

Prosperity of the Jews in Jerusalem. — God's blessing upon
them. — Their pride and rebellion. — Entrance of the
Chaldean soothsayers. — Enmity of Nebuchadnezzar. —
The Babylonians in Jerusalem. — Despoiling of the temple.
— Departure of the enemy with treasures and captives. —
Subjection of the Hebrews in Babylon. — Search by the king
for wise youth. — Choice of the three Hebrews: Hananiah,
Mishael, Azariah. — Their appearance before the king. —
Provision for their needs.

    Gefrægn ic Hebréos éádge lifgean,
    in Hierusalem goldhord dælan,
    cyningdóm habban, swá him gecynde wæs,
    siððan þurh metodes mægen on Moyses hand
5 wearð wíg gifen wígena mænico·
    and hie of Egyptum út áfóron
    mægené miclé: þæt wæs módig cyn,
    þenden hie þý rícé rædan móston,
    burgum wéóldon; wæs him beorht wela,
10 þenden þæt folc mid him hiera fæder wære
    healdan woldon. Wæs him hyrde gód
    heofonríces weard, hálig drihten,
    wuldres waldend, se þam werude geaf
    mód and mihte, metod alwihta,
15 þæt hie oft fela folca feoré gesceódon
    heriges helmum, þára þe him hold ne wæs,

Oð þæt hie wlenco anwôd æt wïnþege
deôfoldædum, druucne geþohtas :
þâ hie ræcræftas âne forlêton,
20   metodes mægenscipe, swâ nô man scyle
his gâstes lufan wið gode dælan !
Þâ gescah ic þâ gedriht in gedwolan lifgan,
Israêla cyn unriht dôn,
wommas wyrcean : þæt wæs weorc gode.
25   Oft hê þâm lêôdum lâre sende
heofonrîces weard hâlige gâstas,
þâ þam werude wîsdôm budon.
Hie þære snytro sôð gelýfdon
lytle hwîle, ôð þæt hie langung beswâc
30   corðan drêâmas êces rædes,
þæt hie æt sîôestan sylfe forlêton
drihtnes dômas, curon deôfles cræft.
Þâ wearð rêðemôd rîces þeôden,
unhold þeôden þâm hê æhte geaf :
35   wîsde him æt frymðe, þâ þe on fruman ær þon
waêron mancynnes metode dýrust,
dugoða drýmust drihtne lêôfost,
herepað tô þære hêân byrig
eorlum elþeôdigum on êðelland,
40   þær Salem stôd searwum âfæstnod,
weallum geweorðod : tô þæs wîtgan fôron
Caldêa cyn tô ceastre forð,
þær Israêla æhta waêron
bewrigene mid weorcum ; tô þâm þæt werod gefôr,
45   mægenþrêât mære mânbealwes georn.
Âwehte þone wælnîð wera aldorfrêâ
Babilones brego on his burhstede
Nabochodonossor þurh nîðhete,
þæt hê sêcan ongan sefan gehygdum,
50   hû hê Israêlum êâðost meahte
þurh gromra gang guman ôðþringan :

gesamnode þâ sûðan and norðan
wælhréöw werod and west faran
herige hæðencyninga tô þære héan byrig:
55　Israêla êðelweardas
lufan lîfwelan, þenden hie lêt metod.
þâ ic êðan gefrægn ealdfêönda cyn
winburh wera : þâ wîgan ne gelŷfdon,
berêâfodon þâ receda wuldor rêâdan goldê,
60　sincê and seolfrê, Salomones templ,
gestrudan gestrêöna under stânhliðum
swilce all swâ þâ eorlas âgan sceoldon,
ôð þæt hie burga gehwone âbrocen hæfdon
þâra þe þam folce tô friðe stôdon.
65　Gehlôdon him tô hûðe hordwearda gestrêön,
fêö and frêös, swilc þær funden wæs,
and þâ mid þâm æhtum eft stôcdon
and gelæddon êâc on langne stð
Israêla cyn on êâstwegas
70　tô Babilonia, beorna unrîm,
under hand hæleð.hæðenum dêman.
Nabochodonossor him on nŷd dyde
Israêla bearn ofer ealle lufen
wæpna lâfe tô weorcþéöwum.
75　Onsende þâ sînra þegna
worn þæs werudes west tô fêran,
þæt him þâra léöda land gehéölde
êðne êðel æfter Ebrêum.
Hêt þâ sêcan sîne gerêfan
80　geond Israêla earme lâfe,
hwilc þære géögoðe gléâwost wære
bôca bebodes, þe þær brungen wæs:
wolde, þæt þâ cnihtas cræft leornedon,
þæt him snytro on sefan secgan mihte,
85　nalles þŷ þe hê þæt môste oððe gemunan wolde,
þæt hê þâra gifena gode þancode,

þe him þær tó duguðe drihten scyrede.
Þá hie þær fundon tó fréâgléâwe
æðele cnihtas and æfæste,
90 ginge and góde in godsæde :
ân wæs Ananias, óðer Azarias,
þridda Misael, metode gecorene.
Þá þrý cómon tó þéðdne foran
hearde and higeþancle, þær se hæðena sæt
95 cyning corðres georn in Caldéa byrig.
Þá hie þam wlancan wîsdóm sceoldon
weras Ebréa wordum cýðan,
higecræft héâne þurh hálig mód.
Þá se beorn bebéâd, Babilone weard
100 swîðmód cyning, sînum þegnum,
þæt þá frumgâras be feore dæde,
þæt þám gengum þrým gâd ne wære
wiste ne wæde in woruldlífe.

II.

*The king's pride and defiance of God. — His unpropitious
dream. — Command to his wise men to tell it. — Being un-
able, he threatens them with death. — Daniel appears before
the king as interpreter. — The king praises and exalts him.*

Þá wæs breme Babilone weard
105 mære and módig ofer middangeard,
egesful ylda bearnum : nó hé æ fremede,
ac in oferhygde æghwæs lifde.
Þá þam folctogan on frumslæpe,
siððan tó reste gehwearf ríce þéðden,
110 com on sefan hwurfan swefnes wóma,
hû woruld wære wundrum getéðd
ungelíc yldum óð edsceafte.

·Wearð him on slæpe sóð gecýðed,
þætte ríces gehwæs róðe sceolde gelimpan,

115 corðan dréamas ende wurðan.
þá onwóc wulfheort, se ær wíngál swæf,
Babilone weard. Næs him blíðe hige,
ac him sorh ástáh swefnes wóman :
nó hé gemunde, þæt him metod wæs.

120 Hét þá tósomne sínra léoda,
þá wiccungdóm wídost bæron,
frægn þá þá mænigeo, hwæt hine gemætte,
þenden reordberend reste wunode :
wearð hé on þam egesan acol worden,

125 þá hé ne wisse word ne angin
swefnes sínes, hét him secgan þéah.
þá him unblíðe andswaredon
déofolwítgan (næs him dóm gearu
tó ásecganne swefen cyninge) :

130 Hú mágon wé swá dygle, drihten, áhicgan
on sefan þínne, hú þe swefnede
oððe wyrda gesceaft wísdóm bude,
gif þu his ærest ne mealht ór áreccan?
þá him unblíðe andswarode

135 wulfheort cyning, wítgum sínum :
Næron ge swá éacne ofer calle men
módgeþances, swá ge me sægdon
and þæt gecwædon, þæt ge cúðon míne
aldorlege, swá me æfre wearð

140 oððe ic furðor findan sceolde,
nu ge mætinge míne ne cunnon,
þá þe me for werode wísdóm bereð !
Ge sweltad déaðé, nymðe ic dóm wite
sóðan swefnes, þæs mín sefa myndgað !

145 Ne meahte þá séo mænigeo on þam meðelstede
þurh wítigdóm wihte áþencean
ne áhicgan, þá hit forhæfed gewearð,

þætte hie sædon swefn cyninge,
wyrda gerŷnu, ôð þæt wîtga cwom
150 Daniel tô dôme, se wæs drihtne gecoren
snotor and sôðfæst, in þæt seld gangan :
se wæs ordfruma earmre lâfe,
þære þe þam hæðenan hŷran sceolde.
Him god sealde gife of heofnum
155 þurh hleôðorcwyde hâliges gâstes,
þæt him engel godes eall âsægde,
swâ his mandrihten gemæted wearð.
Þâ eode Daniel, þâ dæg lŷhte,
swefen reccan sînum freân,
160 sægde him wîslîce wereda gesceafte,
þætte sôna ongeat swîðmôd cyning
ord and ende þæs þe him ŷwed wæs.
Þâ hæfde Daniel dôm micelne,
blæd in Babilonia mid bôcerum,
165 siððan hê gesæde swefen cyninge,
þæt hê ær for firenum onfôn ne meahte,
Babilonie weard, in his breôstlocan.

III.

*The king still defiant. — Raises an idolatrous image in Dura.
— The people bow to it. — The three Hebrews refuse and
are threatened. — They are placed in the fiery furnace. —
Preserved from harm, they rejoice. — The king's anger and
wonder. — The song of Azariah. — Praises God and confesses
the sin of the Jews. — Pleads the covenant and prays for
help. — The angel of deliverance appears and saves them. —
The song of the three Hebrews. — All things praise Jehovah,
the Triune God. — The king and his chiefs take counsel. —
The leader pleads for the youth. — They come out of the
furnace to the king. — The angel ascends. — The king
praises God and favors his servants. — Acknowledges the
wisdom of Daniel.*

Nô hwæðcre þæt Daniel gedôn mihte,
þæt hê wolde metodes mihte gelýfan :
170 ac hê wyrcan ongan weoh on felda,
þam þe déôrmôde Diran hêton,
se wæs on þære þéôde, þe swâ [þrymlíce] hâtte
bresne Babilonige : þære burge weard
ânne manlícan ofer metodes êst
175 gyld of golde gumum ârærde,
forþam hê gléâw ne wæs, gumríces weard
réðe and rædléâs, rihtes [ne gýmde].

Þâ wearð hæleða hlyst, þâ hléôðor cwom
býman stefne ofer burhware.
180 Þâ hie for þam cumble on cnéôwum sæton,
onhnigon tô þam herige hæðne þéôde,
wurðedon wihgyld (ne wiston wræstran ræd),
efnedon unrihtdôm, swâ hyra aldor dyde
mânê gemenged, môdê gefrêcnod :

185 fremde folcmægen, swâ hyra fréâ ærest
    unræd efnde ; him þæs æfter becwom
    yfel endeléân : unriht dyde !
    Þær þrî waéron on þæs þéôdnes byrig
    eorlas Israéla, þæt hie â noldon
190 hyra þéôdnes dôm þafigan onginnan,
    þæt hie tô þam béâcne gebedu rærde,
    þéâh þe þær on byrig bŷman sungon :
    þâ waéron æðelum Abrahames bearn,
    waéron wærfæste, wiston drihten
195 éene uppe ælmihtne.
    Cnihtas cynegôde eûð gedydon,
    þæt hie him þæt gold tô gode noldon
    habban ne healdan ac þone héân cyning,
    gâsta hyrde, þe him gife sealde.
200 Oft hie tô béôte balde gecwædon,
    þæt hie þæs wiges wihte ne rôhton
    ne hie tô þam gebede gebædan mihte
    hæðen heriges wîsa, þæt hie þider hweorfan wolden,
    guman tô þam gyldnan gylde, þe hé him tô gode
            getéôde.
205 Þegnas þéôdne sægdon, þæt hie þære geþeahte næron
    hæftas héran in þisse héân byrig,
    þæt þis [hæðengyld] hérgan ne willað
    ne þisne wig wurðigean, þe þu þe tô wundrum téôdest.
    Þâ him bolgenmôd Babilone weard
210 yrre andswarode ; eorlum onmælde
    grimme þâm gingum and géôcre oncwæð,
    þæt hie gegnunga gyldan sceolde
    oððe þrowigean þréânied micel,
    frécne fŷres wylm, nymðe hie friðes wolde
215 wilnian tô þam wyrrestan, weras Ebréa,
    guman tô þam golde, þe hé him tô gode téôde.
    Noldon þéâh þâ hyssas hŷran lârum
    in hige hæðnum, hogedon georne,

þæt æ godes ealle gelæste
220　and ne âwâcodon wereda drihtnê,
　　ne héanmægen hwyrfe in hæðendôm :
　　ne hie tô fâcne freoðo wilnedan,
　　þéah þe him se bitera déað geboden wære,
　　þâ wearð yrre anmôd cyning :
225　hêt hê [egeslîce] ofn onhætan
　　tô cwale cnihta feorum, forþam þe hie his cræftas on-
　　　　sôcon.
　　þâ hê wæs geglêded, swâ hê grimmost mihte,
　　frêcnê fŷres lîgê, þâ hê þyder folc samnode
　　and gebindan hêt Babilone weard
230　grim and gealhmôd godes spelbodan,
　　hêt þâ his scealcas scûfan þâ hyssas
　　in bælblŷse, beornas ginge.
　　Gearo wæs, se him gêôce gefremede ; þéah þe hie swâ
　　　　grome nŷdde
　　in fæðm fŷres lîge, hwæðere heora feorh generede
235　mihtig metodes weard, swâ þæt mænige gefrunon,
　　hâlige him þær help getêôde. Sende him of héan
　　　　rodore
　　god gumena weard gâst þone hâlgan ;
　　engel in þone ofn innan becwom, þær hie þæt aglâc
　　　　drugon,
　　frêôbearn fæðmum beþeahte under þam fŷrenan hrôfe :
240　ne mihte þéah heora wlite gewemman [ne him wrôht
　　　　ôðfæstan]
　　wylm þæs wæfran lîges, þâ hie se waldend nerede.
　　Hrêôhmôd wæs se hæðena þéôden, hêt hie hraðe
　　　　bærnan :
　　æled wæs ungescêâd micel. Þâ wæs se ofen onhæted,
　　îsen eall þurhglêded : hine þær esnas mænige
245　wurpon wudu on innan, swâ him wæs on wordum
　　　　gedêmed,
　　bæron brandas on bryne blâcan fŷres.

Wolde wulfheort cyning wall onsweallan
íserne ymb æfæste, ðð þæt up gewát
líg ofer léofum and þurh lust geslóh
250 miclê máre, þonne gemet wære.
þá se líg gewand on láðe men
hæðne of hálgum.   Hyssas waêron
blíðemóde, burnon scealcas
ymb ofen ûtan : alet gehwearf
255 téonfullum on teso, þær tó geseah
Babilone brego.   Blíðe waêron
eorlas Ebrêa, ófestum hêredon
drihten on drêáme, dydon swá hie cûðon
ofne on innan aldrê generede.
260 Guman glædmóde god wurðedon,
under þæs fæðme þe geflýmed wearð
frêcne fýres hæto : frêóbearn wurdon
álæten líges ganga ; ne hie him þær láð gedydon :
næs him se swêg tó sorge þon má þe sunnan scíma ;
265 ne se bryne bêót mæcgum, þenden in þam bêóte waêron,
ac þæt fýr scyde tó þám þe þá scylde worhton :
hweorfon þá hæðenan hæftas fram þám hálgum
cnihton ;
wêrigra wlite minsode, þára þe þý worcê gefêógon.
Geseah þá swíðmód cyning, þá hê his sefan ontrêówde,
270 wundor on wíte ágangen ; him þæt wræclíc þúhte :
hyssas hále hwurfon in þam hátan ofne
ealle æfæste þrý [unforbærned].
Him éac þær wæs án on gesyhðe
engel ælmihtiges : him þær ówiht ne derede,
275 ac wæs þær inne ealles gelícost
efne þonne on sumera sunne scíneð
and dêáw-dríás on dæge weorðeð
winde geondsáwen.   þæt wæs wuldres god,
þe hie generede wið þam níðhete.
280 þá Azarias ingeþancum

hléoðrade hálig þurh hâtne líg
dæda georn; drihten hérede
wer womma léâs and þâ word âcwæð:
Metod alwihta! hwæt, þu eart mihtum swîð
285　niðas tô nergenne! is þîn nama mære
wlitig and wuldorfæst ofer werþéóde!
siendon þîne dômas in daga gehwam
sôðe and geswîðe and gesigefæste,
swâ þu éâc sylfa eart [sigores waldend]!
290　syndon þîne willan on woruldspédum
rihte and gerûme, rodora waldend!
Géóca ûser georne nu, gâsta scippend,
and þurh [hyldo] help, hâlig drihten,
nu wê þec for þréâum and for þéó-nýdum
295　and for éâðmédum ârna biddað
lîgé belôgde! Wê þæs lifgende
worhton on worulde, éâc þon wom dyde
ûser yldran for oferhygdum,
bræcon bebodo burhsittende,
300　hâd oferhogedon hâlgan lîfes.
Siendon wê tôwrecene geond wîdne grund
héâpum tôhworfene hylde léâse:
is ûser lîf geond landa fela
fracoð and gefræge folca manegum,
305　þâ usic bewræcon tô þæs wyrrestan
eorðcyninga æhta gewealde,
on hæft heorugrimra, and wê nu hæðenra
þéównéd þoliað: þæs þe þanc sîe,
wereda wuldorcyning, þæt þu ûs þâs wrace téódest!
310　Ne forlæt þu usic, âna éce drihten,
for þâm miltsum þe þec men hlîgað
and for þâm tréówum þe þu tîrum fæst,
niða nergend, genumen hæfdest
tô Abrahame and tô Isaace
315　and tô Jacobe, gâsta scyppend!

þu him þæt gehête þurh hlêôðorcwyde,
þæt þu heora fromcyn in fyrndagum
ícan wolde, þætte æfter him
on cnêôrissum cenned wurde,
320 and sêô mænigeo mære wære
hât tô hebbanne, swâ heofonsteorran
bebûgað brâdne hwyrft ôð þâ brimfaro,
þæs sæfaroða sand geond sealtne wæg
in eare gryndeð, þæt þus his unrîm â
325 in wintra worn wurðan sceolde.
Fyl nu frumspræce, pêâh heora fêâ lifigen,
wlitiga þînne wordewyde and þîn wuldor on ûs!
gecfð cræft and miht, þæt þæt Caldêas
and folca fela gefrigen habbað,
330 þâ þe under heofenum hæðene lifigeað,
and þæt þu âna eart êce drihten,
weroda waldend, woruldgesceafta
sigora settend, sôðfæst metod!
Swâ se hâlga wer hêrgende wæs
335 metodes miltse and his mihta spêd
rehte þurh reorde.   Þâ of roderum wæs
engel ælbeorht ufan onsended,
wlitescŷne wer on his wuldorhaman,
se him cwom tô frôfre and tô feorhnere
340 mid lufan and mid lisse, se þone lîg tôscêâf
hâlig and heofonbeorht hâtan fŷres,
tôswêôp hine and tôswende þurh þâ swîðan miht
ligges lêôman, þæt hyra lîce ne wæs
ôwiht geegled: ac hê on andan slôh
345 fŷr on fêôndas for fyrendædum.
Þâ wæs on þam ofne, þær se engel becwom,
windig and wynsum wedere gelîcost,
þonne hit on sumeres tîd sended weorðeð
dropena drêârung on dæges hwîle,
350 wearmlîc wolcna scûr: swylc bið wedera cyst,

swylc wæs on þam fýre fréan mihtum
hâlgum tô helpe; wearð se hâta lîg
tôdrifen and tôdwæsced, þær þâ dædhwatan
geond þone ofen éodon and se engel mid
355 feorh nerigende, se þær féorða wæs,
Ananias and Azarias
and Misaêl.　Þær þâ môdhwatan
þrŷ on geþancum þéoden héredon;
bædon bletsian bearn Israêla
360 eall landgesceaft écne drihten,
þéoda waldend.　Swâ hie þrŷ cwaédon
môdum horsce þurh gemæne word:
Þe gebletsige, bylywit fæder,
woruldcræfta wlite and weorca gehwilc,
365 heofenas and englas and hluttor wæter!
þâ þe on roderum on rihtre gesceaft
wuniað in wuldre, þâ þec wurðiað,
and þec, ælmihtig, ealle gesceafte,
rodorbeorhtan tunglu, þâ þe ryne healdað,
370 sunna and môna, sundor ânra gehwilc
hêrige in hâde! and heofonsteorran,
déaw and déor scûr, þâ þec dômige
and þec, god mihtig, gâstas lofige!
byrnende fýr and beorht sumor
375 nergend hêrgað, niht somod and dæg!
and þec landa gehwilc, léoht and þéostro,
hêrige on hâde, somod hât and ceald!
and þec, fréa mihtig, forstas and snâwas,
winterbiter weder and wolcenfaru
380 lofige on lyfte! and þec ligetu,
blâce berhtmhwate, þâ þec blestige!
eall eorðan grund, éce drihten,
hyllas and hrusan and héa beorgas,
sealte sæwægas, sôðfæst metod,
385 éastréam ýða and upcyme

waetersprync wylla, þâ þec wurðiað !
hwalas þec hêrigað and hefonfugolas
lyftlâcende ! þâ þe lagostrêamas
wæterscipe wecgað and wildu dêor
390 and nêata gehwilc naman bletsie,
and manna bearn môdum lufiað
and þec Israêla, æhta scyppend,
hêrigað in hâde hêrran sinne !
and þec hâligra heortan cræftas,
395 sôðfæstra gehwæs sâwle and gâstas
lofiað liffrêan, lêan sellende
eallum [æfæstum] êce drihten !
Annanias þec and Adzarias
and Misaêl, metod, dômige
400 brêostgeþancum !   Wê þec bletsiað,
frêa folca gehwæs, fæder ælmihtig,
sôð sunu metodes, sâwla nergend,
hæleða helpend, and þec, hâlig gâst,
wurðiað in wuldre, witig drihten !
405 wê þec hêrigað, hâlig drihten,
and gebedum bremað ! þu gebletsad eart
gewurðad [wide] ferhð ofer worulde hrôf
hêahcyning heofones hâlgum mihtum
lifes lêohtfruma ofer landa gehwilc !
410 þâ þæt ehtode ealdor þêode
Nabochodonossor wið þâm nêhstum
folcgesîðum : þæt êower fela geseah,
þêode mîne, þæt wê þrŷ sendon
geboden tô bæle in byrnende
415 fŷres lêoman !   Nu ic þær fêower men
geseô tô sôðe : nales me sefa lêogeð !
þâ cwæd, se þe wæs cyninges ræswa
wîs and wordglêaw : þæt is wundra sum,
þæt wê þær êagum on lôciað !
420 geþenc, þêoden mîn, þîne gerysna !

ongyt georne, hwâ þâ gyfe scalde
gingum gædelingum ! hie god hêrigað
ânne êcne and ealles him
be naman gehwam on nêðd sprecað,
425 þanciað þrymmes þrîstum wordum,
cweðað hê sîe âna ælmihtig god,
witig wuldorcyning worlde and heofona.
Âban þu þâ beornas, brego Caldêa,
ût of ofne ! nis þæt ôwihtes gôd,
430 þæt hie sîen on þam lâðc leng þonne þu þurfe.
Hêt þâ se cyning tô him cnihtas gangan :
hyssas hearde hŷrdon lâre,
cyrdon cynegôde, swâ hie gecŷðde waêron,
hwurfon hæleð geonge tô þam hæðenan foran :
435 waêron þâ bendas forburnene, þâ him on bânum lâgon,
lâðsearo lêoda cyninges, and hyra lîce geborgen ;
næs hyra wlite gewemmed ne nænig wrôht on hrægle,
ne feax fŷrê beswæled, ac hie on friðe drihtnes
of þam grimman gryre glade treddedon
440 glêâwmôde guman on gâstes hyld.
Þâ gewât se engel up, sêcan him êce drêamas,
on hêâhne hrôf heofona rîces,
hêhþegen and hold hâlgum metode :
hæfde on þam wundre gewurðod, þe] â gewyrhto âhton.
445 Hyssas hêredon drihten for þam hæðenan folce,
sewton hie sôðcwidum and him saêdon fela
sôðra tâcna, ôð þæt hê sylfa gelŷfde,
þæt se wære mihta waldend, se þe hie of þam mirce
          generede.
Gebêâd þâ se bræsna Babilone weard
450 swîðmôd sînum lêodum, þæt se wære his aldrê scyldig,
þe þæs onsôce, þætte sôð wære
mære mihta waldend, se hie of þam morðre âlŷsde.
Âgæf him þâ his lêoda lâfe, þe þær gelædde waêron,
and nahte ealdfêondum, þæt hie âre hæfdon.

455 Wæs heora blæd in Babilone, siððan hie þone bryne
    fandedon ;
    dóm wearð æfter duguðe gecýðed, siððan hie drihtne
    gehýrdon ;
    waéron hyra rædas ríce, siððan hie rodera waldend
    hálig heofonríces weard wið þone hearm gescylde.
    Þá ic sécan gefrægn sóðum wordum,
460 siððan hé wundor onget [worden in ofne]
    Babilones weard þurh bryne fýres,
    hú þá hyssas þrý hátan ofnes
    færgryre fýres oferfaren hæfdon,
    wylm þurhwódon, swá him wiht ne scéðd
465 grim gléda níð, godes spelbodan,
    frécnan fýres, ac him frið drihtnes
    wið þæs egesan gryre aldor gescylde.
    Þá se péðden ongan geþinges wyrcan,
    hét þá tósomne síne léðde
470 and þá on þam meðle ofer menigo bebéad
    wyrd gewordene and wundor godes,
    þætte on þám cnihtum gecýðed wæs :
    Onhicgað nu hálige mihte,
    wíse wundor godes ! we gesáwon,
475 þæt hé wið cwealme gebearh cnihtum on ofne
    lácende líg, þám þe his lof baéron :
    forþam hé is ána écc ælmihtig
    [dugoða] drihten, se þe him dóm forgeaf,
    spówende spéd, þám þe his spel berað :
480 forþon wítigað þurh wundor monige
    hálgum gástum, þe his hyld curon.
    Cúð is, þæt me Daniel dyglan swefnes
    sóðe gesæde, þæt ær swíðe óðstód
    manegum on móde mínra léðda,
485 forþam ælmihtig ácennc gást
    in sefan sende, snyttro cræftas.

IV.

*Still, the king is defiant. — His dream and vision of the great
tree. — Summons his wise men to interpret. — Daniel
summoned. — Interprets the dream as prophetic of the
king's fate. — Pride and downfall of the king. — His reformation and re-establishment. — Acknowledgment of God.
— His public acts and death.*

  Swâ wordum spræc werodes ræswa,
  Babilone weard, siðöan hê beâcen onget,
  swutol tâcn godes : nô þŷ sêl dyde,
490 ac þam æðelinge oferhygd gesceôd,
  wearð him hŷrra hyge and on heortan geþanc
  mâran môdsefan, þonne gemet wære,
  ôð þæt hine mid nŷde nyðor âsette
  metod ælmihtig, swâ hê manegum dêð
495 þâra þe þurh oferhyd up âstigeð.
  þâ him wearð on slæpe swefen ætŷwed,
  Nabochodonossor : him þæt nêh gewearð ;
  þûhte him, þæt on foldan fægre stôde
  wudubeâm wlitig, se wæs wyrtum fæst,
500 beorht on blædum ; næs hê bearwe gelîc,
  ac hê hlifode tô heofontunglum,
  swilce hê oferfæðmde foldan sceâtas,
  ealne middangeard ôð merestreâmas,
  twîgum and telgum, þær hê tô geseah :
505 þûhte him, þæt se wudubeâm wilddeôr scilde,
  âne æte eallum heôlde,
  swylce fuglas eâc heora feorhnere
 • on þæs beâmes blêdum nâme ;
  þûhte him, þæt engel ufan of roderum
510 stîgan cwôme and stefne âbeâd
  torhtan reorde, hêt þæt treow ceorfan

and þá wildéðr on weg fléðn
swylce éac þá fugolas, þonne his fyll cóme ;
hét þonne besnædan seolfes blædum,
515 twígum and telgum and þéh tácen wesan,
wunian wyrtruman þæs wudubéámes
eorðan fæstne, óð þæt eft cyme
gréne bléda, þonne god sylle ;
hét éac gebindan béám þone miclan
520 ærenum clammum and ísernum
and gesæledne in súsl dón,
þæt his mód wite, þæt mihtigra
wíte wealdeð, þonne hé him wið mæge.
Þá of slæpe onwóc (swefn wæs æt ende)
525 eorðlíc æðeling : him þæs egesa stód
gryre fram þam gáste, þe þyder god sende.
Hét þá tósomne síne léðde,
folctogan ; frægn ofer ealle
swíðmód cyning, hwæt þæt swefen bude :
530 nalles þý hé wénde, þæt hie hit wiston,
ac hé cunnode, hú hie cweðan woldon.
Þá wæs tó þam dóme Daniel háten,
godes spelboda : him wæs gæst geseald
hálig of heofonum, se his hyge trymede ;
535 on þam drihtenweard déðpne wisse
sefan sídne geþanc and snytro cræft,
wísne wordcwide. Eft hé wundor manig
metodes mihta for men ætbær,
þá hé secgan ongan swefnes wóman
540 héahheort and hæðen heriges wísa
ealne þone egesan, þe him éðwed wæs,
bæd hine áreccan, hwæt séð rún bude,
hófe háligu word and in hige funde
tó gesecganne sóðum wordum,
545 hwæt se béám bude, þe hé blícan geseah,
and him wítgode wyrda geþingu.

Hê þâ swîgode : hwæðere sôð ongeat
Daniel æt þam dôme, þæt his drihten wæs
gumena aldor wið god scyldig;
550 wandode se wîsa ; hwæðre hê worldê cwæð
ârcræftig âr tô þam æðelinge :
Þæt is, weredes weard, wundor unlytel,
þæt þu gesâwe þurh swefen cuman
heofonhêanc bêam and þâ hâlgan word
555 yrre and egeslîcu, þâ se engel cwæð,
þæt þæt treow sceolde telgum besnæded
foran âfeallan, þæt ær fæste stôd,
and þonne mid dêorum drêamlêas bêon,
wêsten wunian and his wyrtruman
560 foldan befolen fyrstmearc wesan
stille on staðole, swâ sêo stefn gecwæð,
ymb seofon tîda sæde eft onfôn :
swâ þîn blæd lið ! Swâ se bêam gewêox
hêah tô heofonum, swâ þu hæleðum eart
565 âna eallum eorðbûendum
weard and wîsa : nis þe wiðerbreca
man on moldan nymðe metod âna,
se þec âceorfeð of cyningdôme
and þec winclêasne on wræc sendeð
570 and þonne onhweorfeð heortan þîne,
þæt þu ne gemyndgast æfter mandrêame
ne gewittes wâst butan wildêora þêaw,
ac þu lifgende lange þrage
heorta hlýpum geond holt wunast :
575 ne bið þec mæl mête nymðe môres græs
ne rest witod, ac þec regna scûr
wêceð and wreceð swâ wildu dêor,
ôð þæt þu ymb seofon winter sôð gelýfest,
þæt sîe ân metod eallum mannum
580 reccend and rîce, se on roderum is.
Is me swâ þêah willa, þæt se wyrtruma

stille wæs on staðole, swâ séô stefn gecwæð,
and ymb scofon tîde sæde onfênge :
swâ þîn rîce restende bið
585 anwlôh for eorlum, ôð þæt þu eft cymst.
Gehyge þu, fréâ mîn, fæstlîcne ræd :
syle ælmyssan, wes earmra hléô,
þinga for þéôdne, ær þam séô þrah cyme,
þæt hê þec âwcorpe of woruldrîce !
590 Oft metod âlæt monige þéôde
[wéân and] wyrcan, þonne hie woldon sylfe
firene fæstan, ær him fær godes
þurh egesan gryre âldrê gesceôde.
Nô þæs fela Daniel tô his drihtne gespræc
595 sôðra worda þurh snytro cræft,
þæt þæs â se rîca rêcan wolde
middangeardes weard, ac his môd âstâh
héâh fram heortan : hê þæs hearde ongeald !
Ongan þâ gyddigan þurh gylp micel
600 Caldêa cyning, þâ hê ceastre weall,
Babilone burh, on his blæde geseah
Sennera feld sîdne bewindan,
héâh hlifigan, þæt se heretŷma
werede geworhte þurh wundor micel
605 (wearð þâ ânhydig ofer ealle men
swîðmôd on sefan for þære sundorgife,
þe him god sealde gumena rîce
world tô gewealde in wera lîfe) :
Þu eart séô micle and mîn séô mære burh,
610 þe ic geworhte tô wurðmyndum,
rûme rîce ! ic reste on þe,
eard and éðel âgan wylle !
Þâ for þam gylpe gumena drihten
forfangen wearð and on fléâm gewât,
615 Âna on oferhyd ofer ealle men.
Swâ wôd wera on gewindagum

gēocrostne stð in godes wīte,
þāra þe eft lifigende lēode begēte,
Nabochodonossor, siððan him nīð godes
620 hrēð of heofonum hete gesceode.
Seofon winter somod sûsl þrowode
wildēora wēsten winburge cyning.
Þā se earfoðmæcg up lôcade
wildēora gewīta þurh wolcna gang ;
625 gemunde þā on môde, þæt metod wære
heofona hēahcyning hæleða bearnum
āna êce gâst.   Þā hê eft onhwearf
wôdan gewittes, þæs þe hê ær wīde bær
herewôsan hige heortan getenge :
630 þā his gâst âhwearf in godes gemynd,
môd tô mannum, siððan hê metod onget.
Gewât þā earmsceapen eft stôinn
nacod nŷdgenga, nīðgeþafa,
wundorlīc wræcca and wæda lêas
635 mætra on môdgeþanc tô mancynne,
þonne gumena weard in gylpe wæs.
Stôd middangeard æfter mandrihtne,
eard and êðel æfter þam æðelinge
seofon winter samod, swâ nô swiðrode
640 rīce under roderum, ôð þæt se ræswa com.
Þā wæs eft geseted in aldordôm
Babilone weard, hæfde beteran þêaw,
lêohtran gelêafan in liffruman,
þætte god scalde gumena gehwilcum
645 welan swâ wīte, swâ hê wolde sylf.
Ne lengde þā lêoda aldor
wītegena wordcwyde, ac hê wīde bêad
metodes mihte, þæs hê meld âhte ;
sīðfæt sægde sīnum lêodum,
650 wīde wâðe, þe hê mid wilddêorum âtêah,
ôð þæt him frêan godes in gâst becwom·

rædfæst sefa, þa hê tô roderum beseah.
Wyrd wæs geworden, wundor gecýðed,
swefn gesêðed, sûsl âwunnen,
655 dôm gedêmed, swâ ær Daniel cwæð,
þæt se folctoga findan sceolde
earfoðslôas for his ofermêdlan,
swâ hê geornlîce god spellode
metodes mihtum for mancynne.
660 Siððan in Babilone burhsittendum
lange hwîle lâre sægde
Daniel dômas.   Siððan dêora gestô
wildra wærgenga of wâðe cwom,
Nabochodonossor of nîðwracum,
665 siððan weardode wîde rîce,
hêold hæleða gestrêon and þâ hêan burh
frôd foremihtig folca ræswa,
Caldêa cyning, ôð þæt him cwelm gescêod,
swâ him ofer eorðan andsaca ne wæs
670 gumena ænig, ôð þæt him god wolde
þurh hryre hreddan hêâ rîce.

V.

*Reign of Belshazzar. — His downfall and the transfer of the
kingdom to the Medes foretold. — Belshazzar's feast. — The
desecration of the sacred vessels. — Defiance of God. —
The mysterious writing on the wall. — Daniel summoned to
interpret. — His words to the king.*

Siððan þær his aferan êâd bryttedon,
welan, wunden gold in þære wîdan byrig,
ealhstede eorla unwâclîce,
675 hêâh hordmægen, þâ hyra hlâford læg.
þâ in þære þêode âwôc his þæt þridde cnêow,

wæs Baldazar burga aldor,
wéold wera rices, ôð þæt him wlenco gescéod,
oferhyd egle : þâ wæs endedæg,
680 þæs þe Caldéas cyningdôm âhton,
þâ metod onlâh Medum and Persum
aldordômes ymb litel fæc,
lêt Babilone blæd swiðrian,
þone þâ hæleð healdan sceoldon ;
685 wiste hê ealdormen in unrihtum,
þâ þe þý rîcê rædan sceoldon.
Þâ þæt gehogode hâmsittende
Meda aldor, þæt ær man ne ongan,
þæt hê Babilone âbrecan wolde,
690 alhstede eorla, þær æðelingas
under wealla hléo welan brytnedon :
þæt wæs þâra fæstna folcum cûðost,
mæst and mærost, þâra þe men bûn,
Babilon burga, ôðþæt Baldazar
695 þurh gylp grome godes freâsade.
Saêton him æt wîne weallê belocene,
ne onêgdon nâ orlegra nîð,
þéah þe féonda folc féran cwôme
herega gerædum tô þære héahbyrig,
700 þæt hie Babilone âbrecan mihton.
Gesæt þâ tô symble sîdestan dægê
Caldéa cyning mid cnéomâgum :
þær medugâl wearð mægenes wîsa,
hêht þâ [on æht] beran Israêla gestréon,
705 hûslfatu hâlegu on hand werum,
þâ ær Caldéas mid cyneþrymmê
cempan in ceastre clæne genâmon,
gold in Gerusalem, þâ hie Judéa
blæd forbræcon billa ecgum
710 and þurh hléoðor cyme herige genâmon
torhte frætwe, þâ hie tempel strudon,

Salomones seld : swîðe gulpon.

Þâ wearð blîðemôd burga aldor,

gealp gramlîce gode on andan,

715 cwæð þæt his hergas hŷrran waêron

and mihtigran mannum tô friðe,

þonne Israêla êce drihten.

Him þæs tâcen wearð, þær hê tô starude,

egeslîc for eorlum innan healle,

720 þæt hê for lêôdum lygeword gecwæð,

þâ þær in egesan engel drihtnes

lêt his hand cuman in þæt hêâseld,

wrât þâ in wage worda gerŷnu

baswe bôcstafas burhsittendum.

725 Þâ wearð folctoga forht on môde,

acul for þam egesan, geseah hê engles hand

in sele wrîtan Sennara wîte.

Þæt gyddedon gumena mænigeo

hæleð in healle, hwæt seô hand write

730 tô þam bêâcne burhsittendum,

wereдê cômon on þæt wundor seôn :

sôhton þâ swîðe in sefan gehydum,

hwæt seô hand write hâliges gâstes.

Ne mihton ârædan rûncræftige men

735 engles ærendbêc, æðelinga cyn,

ôð þæt Daniel com drihtne gecoren

snotor and sôðfæst in þæt seld gangan,

þam wæs on gâste godes cræft micel.

Tô þam ic georne gefrægn gyfum cêâpian

740 burge weard, þæt hê him bôcstafas

ârædde and ârehte, hwæt seô rûn bude.

Him æcræftig andswarode

godes spelboda glêâw geþances :

Nô ic wið feohsceattum ofer folc bere

745 drihtnes dômas, ne þe dugeðe can !

ac þe uncêâpunga orlæg secge,

worda gerŷnu, þâ þu wendan ne miht.
Þu for anmêdlan in æht bære
hûslfatu hâlegu on hand werum :
750 on þâm ge dêoflu drincan ongunnon,
þâ ær Israela in æ hæfdon
æt godes earce, ôð þæt hie gylp beswâc,
wîndruncen gewit : swâ þe wurðan sceal!
Nô þæt þîn aldor æfre wolde
755 godes goldfatu in gylp beran
ne þŷ hraðor hrêmde, þêah þe here brohte
Israela gestrêon in his æhte geweald,
ac þæt oftor gecwæð aldor þêoda
sôðum wordum ofer sîn mægen,
760 siððan him wuldres weard wundor gecŷðde,
þæt hê wære âna ealra gesceafta
drihten and waldend. se him dôm forgeaf,
unscyndne blæd eorðan rîces :
and þu lîgnest nu, þæt sîe lifgende,
765 se ofer dêoflum dugeðum wealdeð !

NOTES.

NOTES TO EXODUS.

ABBREVIATIONS.

M. = March's Anglo-Saxon Grammar.
The figures refer to sections in the Grammar.
B. = Bouterwek's Cœdmon.
T. = Thorpe's Cœdmon.
MS. = Original Manuscript.
J. = Junius.
G. = Gothic.

I.

1. hwæt! lo! M. 263 (2), 377 (*b*); Beówulf I. 1.—**gefrigen,** have learned by asking. M. 202, 217, 224 (*a*).—**habbath** (habath). M. 222.

2. middangeard, *the middle earth,* between the upper and the lower worlds. (G. midjun-gards.) — **dômas,** *laws, counsels* (dêman, *to judge*). Ex. 20, domjan (G.). — The next five lines may be regarded as appositive and parenthetical.

3. wræclîco, foreign, strange (wraétlîc). — **word-riht,** *just law, oral law.* — **wera** (wair, G.), akin to ware, the plural termination, *inhabitants* (vir). — **cneorissum** (cneow, *knee, relationship*).

4. uproder (uprodor). — **gehwam.** M. 136 (5 *a*).

5. bôte (bêtan). — **tô-bôte,** G. bota.

6. ræd, *counsel, narration* (der. rædan).

7. hæleðum, *heroes, men.* — **gehŷre se þe wille:** this is parenthetical, and similar to that in Scripture: gehŷre, se þe eáran hæbbe tó gehŷranne.

8. weroda (wer), in J. werode; G. wair. — **drihten,** used in composition as intensive; drihten-bealu, weard, beáh. It is sometimes written in the shorter form, driht.

9. cyning, cyn (*race, people*), ing (*descent*), *one of the people.* M. 228, 237 (der. cunnan); G. kuni.

11. alwalda (alwealda, alwaldend). So we have the term Bretwalda. — **æht** (úgan), *ought, own* (G. aigan).

12. leoda (léðdan, *to spring from*), *lewd.*—**aldor** (ealdor).   Ex. 3; 4 : 1–5.

14. folc-toga (here-toga), toga (téðn, *to lead*) = *a leader*, and is chiefly used in compounds.

15. andsacan, in J., andsaca; and as a prep. is intensive, and here has the force of contra.   Ex. 7 : 10.

17. magoræswan, *a kindred chief* (magoræswum, B. and T.).—**feorh,** *life, soul, man* (G. fairhwus).

18. onwist, in J., B., and T., on-wist, *into the abundance.*

21. mid þý, *thereby.*

22. feðndâ, in MS. and J. repeated (G. flands).

23. nægde, *approached, addressed.*   Ex. 3 : 1–6.   Lye makes it poetic for hnigan, *to bow.*

26. eorðan (eardian), (G. airtha).

27. sigerîce, in T., sigê rice.—**sylfes.**   M. 131, 366 (10).

23. yldo (ylda), (G. alds), Eng. eld.

31. gewurðodne, M. 401 (*a*).

33. iu-gêre (gêarâ, gêare), *of yore.*   M. 251 (1).—**ingere** (MS., B., and T.).

34. ealdum wîtum, Thorpe translates as if wîsum.

36. feledreamas (B. and T.).

38. frêcne, *boldly, severely.*   Ex. 12 : 29.

39. The omission of the colon is better.   If not, a verb may be understood.

40. drysmyde (ðrysmede), (þrysmôde); dryrmde (B., T., and MS.). (In Beowulf, drysmað, 1375.)

41. dugoð (dugan).

42. Ex. 12 : 30.

44. waêron, understood (lâðsið, MS.).—**grætan** (grêtan).—**leode,** nom. pl.

45. frêond, MS.   Ex. 12 : 36.

46. heofon, *lamentation.*   In T., heaven.

49. swâ, may have a relative force, *who,* G. swa.—**þæs:** the reading, þæt (B.), is better.—**missera,** *half-years, seasons.*

51. wîde-fer(h)ð, *large-minded, spacious, perpetually.*

52. metod, *the measurer* (metan).

55. magoræswa, in MS. and J., magoræwa.

57. Grein suggests **leodgeard.**

59. Gûðmyrce, in T., gûð-myrce, *hostile frontier* (ælmyrean).

61. môrheald (môr heald (heðld), T.); the mountain held their tents.

63. (God) then commanded (hêht). — **tîrfæstne,** Tîr (tŷr), *glory, power.* As a prefix it denotes something superlative.

65–6. The passage is thought to be hopelessly obscure. — **bearhtmê,** *sound, tumult* (clangor of music). — **æl-fere,** *with all the host* (æl-faru, æl-fær); el-fære (Grein). Ex. 12 : 37 ; 13 : 20.

67. mearclandum, T.

II.

68. geneðdon, genŷddon (T., B.).

69. Sigelwara, of the Sunfolks, *Ethiopians.*

71. hâtum heofoncolum, instrumental after brûne.

72. fær, *sudden, severe,* used as a prefix.

75. weder-wolcen, *heavy* (threatening) *cloud.* Ex. 13 : 21.

77–8. In Thorpe, *quenched was the flame-fire with heat* (hatê) ; G. heito.

78. hæleð (as). M. 74 (1 *a*).

79. dægscealdes, *pillar of cloud.* In Lye, dægsceades ; G. dags, skadus.

81. seglê (B. and T., swegle).

87. Some lines are here omitted by the copyist. Ex. 14 : 2.

91. cwom, M. 200 (G. kwiman).

92. wîcsteal, *a camp, place of rest;* wîc is much used as a termination.

93. fôran (fóron), (G. gaggan).

94. twegen, M. 141 (G. twai), Eng. twain.

95. æghwæðer, M. 135, 136 (5 *b*).

96. Ex. 14 : 19.

98. môdes rôfan, M. 313.

99. hebban, M. 207 (*d*) ; Eng. heave, heaven. — **hlûdum stefnum,** G. hafjan.

102. folce, appositive with him.

104. lîftweg; in MS., B., and T., lifweg.

105. segl sîðe; in B. and T., swegl-sîðc.

106. Some editors suggest **fold.**

109–11. March reads, " Strange after sunset (there) took care over the people with flame to shine a burning pillar."

113. sceado, M. 100 (*a*) ; MS. sccaðo.

114–15.. *The falling night shadows might not near hide the gloom.* — **bearn** (barn).

117–19. By reason of defects in the original text, the construction

here is difficult: **him . . . ferhð,** *their soul.* — Ô **fêrclammê** (oferclam-
mé) **getwæfde** (gctwæf), *with sudden peril distract.* — **wêstengryrê(e)**
may be nom. or inst.

121. bæl-egsan, M., B., and T., bell.

122. hâtan, M. 362 (1). — **in þam** (B. and T.).

123. hê (lige).

124. hyrde(n), M. 179.

131. bêtân (béton, B. and T.).

132. æfter beorgum, *over the hill slopes.*

134. þam (þan). Ex. 14 : 2.

III.

136. ôht inlende, *domestic fear.* Ex. 14 : 10.

137. wræcmon, *the fugitive* (Israel).

138. lâstweard, *successor, persecutor* (Pharaoh).

139. ôht-nied, *persecution* (on nied, B. and T.).

140. wean, may be taken as appositive with ôht-nied.

141. There are omissions here in MS. — **ge[tiðode],** *granted.*

142. hê, omitted in B. and T.

143. miceles, M. 251 (1); (G. mikils).

145. ymb andwîg (ântwig), *about a rod* (Aaron's), (ân-wîg). Ex. 7 : 10.

148. heaðo wylmâs, *battle waves, bitter feuds.* This prefix is intensive, and is similar to gûð, beade, hild. It denotes war. — **heortan
getenge,** *heavy at heart.*

149. mânum trêowum, *with false faith.*

151. Thorpe makes **hê** collective (hie, Grein).

154. him refers to the warriors. — **eorla, ortrýwe,** M. 254 (1).

156. ongangan, participial use of the infinitive. In B. and T., Faraonis. Ex. 14 : 10.

158. In T. and B. this line is placed after 160. The order of the text in Grein is better.

161. hrêopon (hwrêopon, T.).

162. [hræfen gôl], omitted in B. and T. In B. (gûðes gifre).

164. wælceasega, *the raven.*

165. æfenlêoð.

166–7. *The slaughter renowned ones awaited* (beodan = bidon) *on the
track of the foe, the destruction* (fyl) *of the host.* In B. and T., ful; G. beidan. Thorpe's rendering of this passage is all wrong.

169. genæged, *subdued* (gehæged, B. and T.).

171. *measured the mile paths with the legs of (the) horses, advanced.*

172. sigecyning (segncyning), *king of Egypt.*

176. wælhlencan scêoc (hwæl, T.).

178. feönd onsêgon (freönd onsigon (onsawon), B. and T.).

179. eagum (eagan).

181. heorowulfås (here, B.; heora, T.).

184. þûsendo, M. 141; G. þusendi. — tîr-eadigra (tîrca-digra, B.).

186. on þæt eade riht, "chosen (âlesen) to that rich inheritance" (Grein). "To that important duty" (Carpenter). The reading of Thorpe, on þam eorð-rîce, is needless.

190. ingemen, *in common.* Grein and others suggest -ing (geong).

191. cûðost, cûð eft gebâd (B.); cûð oft gebâd (T.).

192. tô hwæs hægstealdmen, *to the leaders of which* (heapes).

193. bæron, *offered themselves.*

194. eorp werod, *the Egyptians.* — êcan læddon (sê anlæddon, B. and T.).

204. It is not essential that **werud** should refer to Israel.

206. gelâðe, *the hostile.* In T. and B., gelâde, *the way.*

IV.

209. on healfa gehwam, *on either side.* — hettend (as), M. 74 (1 *a*).

213. weân, nom. pl. of the adj.

215. mâran mægenes, gen. after bâd.

216. uhttîd, *before dawn* (3 to 6 A.M.).

219. cîgean, depends on bebeâd.

222. bŷman (bênum, T.).

224. teônhete, *dire hate.*

225. on þam forðherge, *in the van.*

226. rôfa [rôfra].

227. æðeles (æðelan, B. and T.).

233. waċe (wac, B. and T.), object of grêtton.

237. feönd(a).

239. linde lærig, *shield rim.* (The linden shields, T.) — swor (spor), (sweor).

242. gif (git). — môdheapum (hæpum), *the wise.*

243. be wæstmum, *according to strength.* — wîg (wigan).

245-6. þan (þæt) gegân mihte, omitted in B. and T. — fêng, may be taken as an acc., *handling.*

248. fûs forðwegas(es), *ready for departure.* M. 315.

249. bidou (bufon, B.; buton, T.).

250. sîðboda, *pillar of fire.*

V.

253. beot-hâta (beo-hata), *surety, leader.*

255. môdiges, *chief.*

259. Ex. 14 : 13.

265. ægulau, eglian.

266. ne willað ondrædan, *dread not* (M. 440).

272. sigora gesynto, *fruits of triumph.*

277. leod (þeod(en)).

279. leofost, voc. G. lubo.

281. tâne (tâcne, B. and T.). Ex. 14 . 21, 27; 14 : 16.

282. ôfstum, M. 251 (1).

283. Some texts omit and. Ex. 14 : 29. Grein retains it in the sense of a preposition, for a wall.

287. famige (fage, B. and T.).

289–90. sælde (scalte). — sûðwind, appos. with blæst. — **brim** (bring, T.).

291. sæcir, *the ebb.* — spân (spâv). — sôðgere, *very well.*

293. ær glâde, *ere sunset;* glade, adv., *friendly.* — eorlas, voc.

294. weorðen, *escape.* G. wairþan.

298. wrætlîcu (wræclîcu).

304. âudægne fyrst, M. 295 (a).

305. ŷða weall, omitted in B. and T.

307. hîgê (MS., hi), (B., hie).

308. læste near, *nearer its close.* The text is here defective.

309. sunges (sauces, B. and T.); G. suggws. Ex. 14 : 22.

313. orette (onette). — uncûð gelâd, M. 295 (a).

321. leon (leor).

322. After maêst the verb is supplied.

323. hŷnðu, M. 100 (a).

324. be him lifigendum, *while living.* M. 334.

326. þeoda aênigre, *against any nation.* — þracu (þraca, T.).

328. waêpna, gen. after môdige. G. wepna. There is seen here a succession of nominatives.

331. môdgade (ôde), *moved proudly.*

333. sæwîcinge (sæwicingas, B. and T.); G. saiws.

335. hê, Reuben.

339. ead and æðelo, *wealth and rank.* — earu (ge-earu, gearu).

340. forð, omitted by some.

343. gûðcyst (gûðcyste).

344. dæg-wôma, *cloud.*

345. begong (gin, B.), omitted in T.

350. for, omitted (B. and T.), folcum.

353. The interpolated poem begins here. fæder, M. 100 (*f*), (fadar, G.).

354. landriht geþah, parenthetical.

357. After sum the verb is understood.

359. orðancum, the prefix or is used both privatively and intensively.

361. fæðeræðelo gehwæs, *the ancestry of each.*

VI.

362. niwe (niðe).

363. þrim, M. 141; G. þreis.

364. dren-flôda (T.).

365. þe, M. 380.

368. mînê gefrægê, *as I have heard.* So in Bêowulf.

370. êce lâfe (B. and T.).

374. saêlida þon(ne).

380. se, M. 368 (*b*). Se him, M. 381 (2).

385. Some prefer stîgan.

392. alh (G. alhs), alhn (J.).

394. gefrægost, *most famed.*

399. A line thrown in. Supposed that Cain is referred to.

401. beorn, used chiefly in poetry.

405. tô lâfe (T.) is not admissible.

410. þonne, þonne.

411. eaferan (B. and T.).

412. reodan applies to ecgum rather than to Isaac.

413. god (B. and T.).

422. seo, *which.*

424. aldre (B. and T.).

431. ne (T.).

433. weard, omitted in B. and T.

436. yldo (B. and T.), G. aiws.

438. þæs, M. 252 (II).

443. in-geþeode (inca þeode).

445. A blank is found here in MS. This entire section constitutes an interpolated poem going over the Bible history from Noah to Isaac. It would find a fitting place in Genesis.

VII.

History of Israel is here resumed.

453. herebleaðe, *the panic-stricken*, bliðe (T.). Ex. 14:25, 27, 28.

454. gehnáp (genap).

458. módgóde, *raged*.

466. saês æt ende (B. and T.).

469. Lye reads nere (*refuge*). —forðganges nef, *the tide's neap* (T.).

470-5. See Thorpe's Cædmon, p. 207. —barenoden (B. and T.). — on, omitted (B. and T.). —waðema, *stream, wave stream.* —gewuna may be taken as an adj. agreeing with saê. —fáh feðc-gást, *hostile visitor, (foot-guest).* —fáh wæs se gæst (B.), (ge-(h)ncðp). See Carpenter's Grammar, p. 169.

479. módge (mód). G. muns.

487. helpendra(n).

488. hê, *the stream.*

490. on sleap (steap, T.).

491. witród (witód).

498. on bógum (B. and T.).

499. móde waêga (B. and T.).

501. onfêond.

502. grund, omitted in B. and T.

503. þæt wæs (B. and T.).

504. hilde gesceâdan, *decide the battle;* huru (B. and T.).

513. spilde, omitted in B. and T.

514. ágeat, *destroyed.* —þe, for hie (T.). Exclamatory, They against God warred!

VIII.

518. dægweorc nemuað(eð), *they call it* (the decalogue) *the day guide* (of life).

524. gin fæsten (T.).

525. rún (G. runa), rúnian, *to whisper.* —geregenod (B.).

528. Words omitted: That we seem not (forgetful).

529. metódes (B. and T.).

531. lýf(t) (lyst, B.).

534. healdeð (B. and T.).

538. regn, an intensive prefix, regn-heard.

545. is, omitted (B. and T.).

555. ufon (B. and T.).

569. gefeon (B. and T.).

570. hit (hie).

573. herge, omitted (T.). — þâm hildfrumun (B.).

576. wîfon ôðrum, *the women in turn.* Ex. 15.

585. madmas (B. and T.).

586. sceo(d) (B. and T.).

589. driht folca, emphatic prefix. — maêst (MS. mæ), (G. maist(s)).

Of the forty chapters of Exodus given by Moses, Cædmon paraphrases but a few, and even here the poet follows the sacred narrative much less closely than in Daniel. As far as the authoritative text is concerned, the first fifteen chapters of the history may be said to be the only ones referred to by the author. He dismisses the subject as the people stand upon the farther shore of the Red Sea with the promised land before them. It is also noticeable that incidents and facts are introduced which are not found in the Biblical record, such as the precise order of march through the Red Sea, the special valor of the warlike bands selected to oppose Pharaoh, and many minute statements as to the pillar of cloud and of fire. The most important references by the poet to the text of Exodus have been given in the course of the Notes.

NOTES TO DANIEL.

I.

  1. Hebréôs, M. 101. — **eadge,** adverbial in force.

  2. dælan, dæljan (G.)

  3. gecynde, *natural, agreeable.*

  5. wîg, *martial force.* — **manleo, same as** menigeo, menigu.

  7. môdig cyn, *a haughty race.*

  8. rædan, *rule,* not to be confounded with the strong verb raêdan, *to counsel.*

  9. burgum, beorgan, *to protect.*

  10. him, God. — **fæder,** gen. pl. M. 87.

  14. môd, *courage.*

  15. feorê, M. 301 (*a*); *idiomatic usage.*

  16. helmum, *chieftains.*

  19. ân forlêton (T.). — **æcræftas,** *legal statutes.*

  22. þege driht (MS. and J.). — **hweorfan** (T. and B.); M. 204 (*b*).

  24. weorc, *grief.*

  25. lâre, acc. pl., appos. with gâstas. This is preferable to Thorpe's rendering in the dative.

  28. sôð, *truly.* G. sunja.

  29. me (MS. and J.), *for.* — **hie, lytlê hwîle,** acc. of time. M. 295 (*a*).

  34. þéôdne (T.). — **þâm þe** (T.).

  35. wîsðe, MS.; wîsode, B.

  37. dugoða dŷrust (MS., B., and T.).

  38. herepoð (MS.), object of wîsde.

  41. to þæs (ceastre).

  42. ceastre, M. 90. The text is more or less defective from 35 to 42.

  44. to þâm (weorcum).

  45. mân bealwes georn, *zealous of evil.*

  46. wælnlð, *fatal hate.*

  52. sûðan and norðan, M. 252 (*b*).

53. hêt, may be in place after faran.

55. Thorpe makes cðelweardas appos. with hæðencyningas.

56. lufan = lufon, from leófan.

57. þâ éac (MS., T., and B.).

64. tô friðe, *in peace.*

66. feâ (MS., T., and B.).—freos (freogas), (frigas), *treasure and captives.*

73. ôtor (MS. and T.), ûton (B.).

74. wæpna lâfe, *the survivors.*

77. leóde (MS. and B.).

82. This line probably refers to lâfe (l. 80).

88. Thorpe suggests freân. So (B.).

90. in gôd sæde (T.), *of good race.*

96. þam wlancan (cyninge).

97. cyðdon (MS. and T.).

101. Thorpe translates, "What the princes before did." The line is obscure. The sense is complete without it.

II.

110. com hwurfan, *came passing.*

112. ôð edsceafte, *until renewal.*

118. wôma (MS. and T.).

119. metod = mætod, *dreamed.* May also be p.p. of metian, *appointed* (in his dream).

122. hine gemætte, M. 290 (*a*).

123. reord berend : Grein prefers this in nom. pl.

131. þe swefnede, M. 290, 299.

133. his, connected with ôr.

137. môdgeþances, M. 321.

139. aldorlege, *life's destiny.*—æfter (MS. and T.); G. aftra.

141. ne ge, MS.

142. bereð, used as berað.

148. sædon, in the sense of sæden.

160. wŷrda (T. and B.).

III.

169. hê, *the heathen king.*

171. þam, dative of attraction.

172. þeóde, *province.*

173. burh weardas (B.).

176. forð̃am þe (T.).

177. The text is here defective.

179. There are two terminal forms : ware-â, pl. m.; warv-e, f. sing.

189. þâ þe (T.), M. 380, 381.

191. râerdon (B. and T.), (rærden).

192. on herige (MS. and T.); G. harjis.

193. að̃elum, *in nature.*

196. cynegôde, *gentle, noble.* — cûð̃ gedydon, *made known.*

197. gyld (B.). — him is not essential to the reading. It may refer to the youths or to the king.

200. tô bêôte, *moreover.* Eng., to boot.

202. gebaêdan (T.), *persuade.*

205. waêron (T. and B.). — hie, appos. with hæftas.

206. hêâran (MS., B., and T.), *proud captives.* — hêran, *to honor* (the idol).

207. hêgan (MS.); hêrgan = hêran. In lines 205–7 the text as it reads is best.

214. woldon (T. and B.), (wolden).

216. gylde (B.).

219. gelæston (T.), gelæsten (B.).

221. ne þan mægen hwyrfe, T. (high course). Grein refers this to the captive Jews. Hwyrfe is then viewed as a verb.

222. wilnedan (wilneden).

227. wæs gelaêded (T. and B.). — hê, *the oven.*

232. genge (T. and B.).

233. þêah þe [he], *the king.* — se = seþe, *he who.*

234. fŷr-lîges (T.).

236. haliga (T.). — se, *understood.*

240. Words in brackets omitted by T. and B.

243. ungescêâd, used adverbially.

244. hine after innan.

247. onstealle, MS.; onstellan, B.; onsteallan, T. Grein admits that his rendering is here objectionable.

255. on teso, Thorpe translates, "on the right." Grein renders, "destruction."

263. gange (T. and B.). Grein makes it in the gen. pl. after âlæten.

266. ac þæt fŷr fŷrscyde (MS. and J.); fyrsian, *to remove* (Dietrich).

267. hâlgan (B.). — hweorfon = hwurfon. — cnihton = cnihtum.

268. þâ þe (B.). — gefægon (T. and B.).

274. ælmihtiges (Godes or Drihtnes).

277. deâwdrepan, B.; deâwdripaš, T.

282. dædum, Codex Ex.

289. An interpolated line, T.   Not in Ex. MS.

294. þrêa-nŷdum (T. and B.). — þearfum, Codex Ex.

296. belegde (T.).

297. dydon, Codex Ex.

299. burhsittendum (MS. and J.).

300. hâd, *condition.*

304. gefræge, *notorious, infamous.*

305. nu þu usic bewræc, Codex Ex.; þa us êc, T.

306. æht-gewealde (B.), Codex Ex.   This would be in apposition with usic, and be rendered, *a possession.*

311. hrûgaჯ (B. and T.), *incline.*   Thorpe favors this rendering. Grein reads hli(ŷ)gaჯ, *call upon, invite.*

321. hâd (B.), appos. with manigeo.   Grein interprets in the sense of promise (gehât). — hebbanne = hæbbanne, *to reckon.*

323. swâ waroჯe sond, Codex Ex. — þass sæfaroჯa sand, *the sand of whose waves.*

324. ŷჯe geond ear grund, Codex Ex.; eargrynde, B. — his, *of them, God's people.* — unrîma, T.

328. þæt þâ (T.).

343. leoma(n) (B.). — lîges (B.).

350. cyst, *bounty.*

364. woruld sceafta wuldor, Codex Ex.

366. rihtne (T.).

370. sunne and monan, Codex Ex. — sundor ânra gehwilc, *each one, separately.*

372. dômige = dômigen.

373. lofigen.

379. folcen faru (T.).

380. lôfigen.

381. blestige = bletsigen.

393. þînne (hŷra), T. — in hâde, *in* (their) *degree.*

399. dômige = dômigen.   This use of the sing. subj. for the plural is frequent in Daniel.

404. wurჯaჯ (B.).

407. gewurჯaჯ (MS. and J.). — ferhჯ(e) (B. and T.).

409. Defective text, T.

410. ealde (B. and T.), *ancient nation.*   Grein's text is better.

413. þeჯde mîne, *my lords.* — syndon (T.).

416. selfa (B. and T.).

417. cwad = cwæð. G. kwiþan.

422. gædelinge, B. — um, T.

429. nis hit (B.).

430. leng, M. 124.

435. benne (T.). — him, dative of possession after bânum.

436. lâðsearo, appos. with bendas.

446. stêpton (B. and T.). — hine (T.).

447. hê, *the king.*

451. se (B. and T.).

454. nahte (nâgan), hnahte allowed. Dietrich reads rahte (reccan). — hæfdon = hæfden.

467. wið þæs egesan gryre, *against the fear of terror.*

468. geþinges wyrcan, *to form an assembly.*

476. wið understood.

479. his spel berað, *his words observe.*

480. monig (B. and T.).

497. him þæt nêh gewearð, *that came near to him* (greatly moved him).

IV.

500. him (T.), after gelîc.

506. heolde, *a lair.*

508. namon (T.), nâmen. G. niman.

518. wille (T.).

521. in sûsl dôn, *to cast into torment.*

523. mæge, *may prevail.*

535. wesan, supplied after wisse.

538. mihte (B.), mihtum (T.).

542. hine, *Daniel.*

546. hwæt, supplied after and.

554. heanne (B. and T.).

562. and ymb (T.). — sædê, instrumental after onfôn.

563. bið (B.). Grein makes lið = ligeð.

568. In this and the two following lines the present tense of the verb has the force of the future.

571. gemyndgast, MS.

575. mæl-mête (T.).

582. wære (T.).

588. þinga, *pray.*

591. [weân and], inserted by Grein. — **wyrcan,** *to act* (with impunity).

596. reccan (B. and T.).

600. weôld (B. and T.); G. waldan.

603. heâh [burh] (B. and T.).

607. rîce, in appos. with sundorgife.

609. earð (MS. and T.).

616. woð = wað (B. and T.), *a way, wandering.* Grein supplies hê (*the king*) after swâ.

618. berehte (T.).

623. locode (T.).

628. þaêr þe (B.).

633. geþafian (B.), geþolian (T.).

658. ôfstlîce (B.). Grein reads, god-spellôde (godspellian).

661. lâre, inst. used adverbially, *wisely.*

V.

675. læg, *perished.*

682. ym (MS. and J.). — lîtel fæc, M. 295.

684. þâ, Medes and Persians.

695. frea sæde (T.).

701. sîdestan = siðestan.

710. hleoðor cwyde (T.), *prophecy.*

711. beorhte.

718. þæt (T.).

740. burhgeweardas (B. and T.).

741. ârehte, M. 189 (c).

743. gléâw geþances, M. 313.

748. bere (B. and T.).

756. hê (T.). This change seems to be essential.

759. ofer sîn mægen, *among his army.*

765. se (þe).

Cædmon's Daniel is such a faithful paraphrase of the first five chapters of that book that special scriptural references need not be given as in Exodus.

REFERENCES.

Much valuable information as to Cædmon and his Paraphrase is given in Bede's *Ecclesiastical History* (c. 4); Wright's *Biographia Brittanica Literaria;* in Kemble (*Bibliotheca Anglo-Saxonica,* 1837); in Dietrich (*Haupt's Zeitschrift,* Bd. 10); and in Greverus. Additional aid may be found in Ten Brink's *History of Early English Literature;* in such histories as Turner's, Morley's, Craik's, and Warton's. The student may also be referred to modern German periodicals for valuable articles on points in question. The two most important of these are *Die Englische Studien* and *Anglia.* In this latter one, especially, useful papers may be found by Ebert, Wülcker, and others, on Exodus and on the Cædmon — Milton question. Such authors as Balg, Sandras, Bosanquet, Disræli, Stein, and Watson may also be consulted. A full bibliography of Cædmon will be given by the editor of Genesis.

GLOSSARY.

GLOSSARY.

The gen. sing. and the gender of each noun are given, as also the three main parts of each verb. For the convenience of students using March's Grammar the different declensions and conjugations are indicated by the appropriate figures 1, 2, etc. Any accidental omissions of words may be supplied by a reference to Bosworth or Grein. M. and G. are to be interpreted as in Notes. Any other contractions or references will be easily understood by the student. As stated in the Preface, our object has been to make the Glossary as brief as is consistent with clearness.

A (Æ).

â, adv., *ever, aye.*

âba(o)nnan, bên, ba(o)nnen (5), *to order, summon, proclaim.* M. 100.

abêôdan, bêâd, boden (3), *to bid, announce, command.*

Abraham, es, m., *Abraham.*

abrecan, bræc, brecen (1), *to break, destroy.*

abre(g)dan, bræ(g)d, bro(g)den (1), *to remove, withdraw.*

abrêôtan, brêât, broten (3), *to bruise, destroy.*

ac, conj., *but.* G. ak.

aceorfan, cearf, corfen (1), *to cut off, separate.*

acl, adj., *clear, resounding.*

acol, adj., *timid, affrighted.*

âcweðan, cwæð, cweden (1), *to say, declare, answer.* G. kwiþan.

âdfŷr, es, 1, n., *a pile-fire, fire of sacrifice.*

adrencan, te, ed (6), *to submerge, drown.*

adrincan, dranc, druncen (1), *to quench, to be drowned.* G. driggkan.

Adzarias, as, m., *Azarias.*

að, es, 1, m., *an oath.* G. aiþis.

aðswar, es, 1, m., *an oath swearing, an oath.*

âe, âe, f. (irreg.), *a law* (pl., *rites*). M. 100.

æcræft, es, 1, m., *a legal statute, law craft.*

æðele, adj., *noble, excellent.*

æðele, es, 1, m., *a noble.*

æðeling, es, 1, m., *a prince, chief.*

æðelo, indec., *nobility, rank.*

æf(a)est, adj., *devout, religious.*

(a)efen, es, 1, m., *even, evening.*

æfenlêôd(ð), es, 1, n., *an evening song.*

æflâst, es, 1, m., *a straying, wandering.*

æfre (æfer), adv., *ever, always.* G. aiw.

(a)efter, prep., *after, according to.*

æghwâ, es, adj. pro., *whoever, each one.*

æghwæðer, es, adj. pro., *each, both.*

æghwilc, es, adj. pro., *every one, each one, every.*

ægnian, ôde, od (6), *to own, hold.*

æht, e, 2, f., *property, possessions.*

ælbeorht, adj., *all bright, very bright.*

æled(t), es, 1, m., *fire.*

ælfero (faru), e, 2, f., *an entire army, a host.*

a(e)lmihtig, adj., *almighty.* G. all-mahteigs.

ælmy(o)sse, an, 4, f., *alms, alms-giving.*

aêr, adv., *ere, earlier* (aêrôr, aêrest).

ærdæg, es, 1, m., *early day, dawn.*

ær-déað, es, 1, m., *premature death, early death.*

æron, adj., *brazen* (ær).

ærend, e, 2, f., *an errand, a message.* G. airus.

ærendbôc, e, 2, f., *a message, letter.*

æt, prep., *at, near, by.*

æt, es, 1, m., *meat, food.* G. mats.

ætberan, bær, be(o)ren (1), *to bear out, show, produce.*

ætgædere, adv., *together.*

Æthan, es, *Etham.* M. 101.

ætniman, nam, numen (1), *to deprive, take from.*

ætŷwan, de, ed (6), *to show, reveal* (ŷwian, ôde, od).

Afæran, de, ed (6), *to frighten, terrify.*

Afæstinan, ôde, od (6), *to fasten, strengthen.*

Afaran, fôr, faren (4), *to depart, go out of.*

Afeallan, féol, feallen (5), *to fall, fall down.*

afera, an, 4, m., *a son, descendant* (eafora).

Afrisc, adj., *African.*

Agan, âhte (6), (irreg.), *to own, possess.* G. aigan. M. 212.

Agangan, g(ê)ong, gangen (5), *to happen, occur.* M. 208 (b).

agen, adj., *own.*

Agend, es, 1, m., *an owner, master, lord.*

Agéotan, géat, goten (3), *to pour out, destroy.*

Agifan, geaf (gæf), gifen (1), *to restore, deliver.* M. 149.

Agitan, geat, giten (1), *to know, perceive, understand.*

aglâc, es, 1, n., *grief, torment.*

Ahebban, hôf, hafen (4), *to raise, exalt.* G. hafjan.

Ahi(y)cgan, hog(ô)de (hygde), hogod (6), *to search, explore, think out.*

Ahleapan, hléop, hleapen (5), *to leap up, out, to leap.*

Ahweorfan, hwearf, hworfen (1), *to turn aside, to turn.*

Ahŷdan, de, ed (6), *to hide, conceal.*

Alædan, de, ed (6), *to lead out, withdraw.*

Al(a)êtan, lêt, laêten (5), *to allow, release.*

ald (eald), adj., *old.* G. alþeis.

aldor, es, 1, m., *an elder, prince.*

aldor, e, 2, f., *life.*

aldordôm, es, 1, m., *seat of power, sovereignty.*

aldorfréa, an, 4, m., *a high lord, chief.*

aldorleg(e), es, 1, m., *life's future, fate, death.*

Alesan, læs, lesen (1), *to choose, gather.*

alh, es, 1, m., *a palace, shrine, temple.*

alhstede, es, 1, m., *a hall-stead, palace.*

all, see eall. G. alls.

alwalda, an, 4, m., *a ruler over all, God.*

alwiht, e, 2, f., *every creature, all people.*

Alŷfan, de, ed (6), *to allow, suffer.*

Alŷsan, de, ed (6), *to free, release.*

ân, num. adj., *one, alone, only.* G. ains.

anbîd, es, 1, n., *a delay, expectation.*

and, conj., *and.*

anda, an, 4, m., *hate, envy.*

ân-dæge, adj., *a space of one day, daily.*

andsaca, an, 4, m., *a denier, opposer.*

andswarian, ôde, od (6), *to answer, reply.*

andwîg, es, 1, m., *a battle, repulse.*

anga, adj., *sole, own.*

ân-getrum, es, 1, n., *one host, a great number, an array.*

angi(y)n, es, 1, n., *a beginning, attempt.*

ânhydig, adj., *resolute, single-minded, obstinate.*

anlædan, de, ed (6), *to lead on.*

anmedla, an, 4, m., *pride, presumption.*

anmôd, adj., *unanimous, wilful, one.*

ânpað, es, 1, m., *one path, a narrow path.*

anwadan, wôd, waden (4), *to enter, invade.*

anwlôh, adj., *unadorned, waste.*

âr, e, 2, f., *glory, honor, wealth.*

âr, es, 1, m., *a legate, messenger.*

ârædan, de, ed (6), *to read, interpret.*

âræman, de, ed (6), *to raise, lift up; also, reflexive.*

âræran, de, ed (6), *to rear, extol, raise aloft.*

ârcræftig, adj., *reverend, honorable.*

ârêafian, ôde, od (6), *to tear away, withdraw, divide.*

ârec(c)an, e(a)hte, e(a)ht (6), *to declare, explain.*

ârîsan, râs, rîsen (2), *to arise.* G. urreisan.

âsælan, de, ed (6), *to tie, bind.*

âsceppan, scêôp, sc(e)apen (5), *to give, appoint.*

âsecgan, sægde (saêde), sægd (saêd) (6), *to tell, explain, declare.* M. 209.

âsettan, te (6), *to set down, place, fix.* G. gasatjan.

âstîgan, stâh, stîgen (2), *to ascend, arise.*

âswebban, efede, efed (6), *to blot out, destroy.*

âteôn, teâh, togen (3), *to draw up, move away.*

atol, adj., *dire, foul.*

aþenc(e)an, þohte, þoht (6), *to discover, devise.*

âwa, adv., *ever, alway.*

âwacan, wôc, wacen (4), *to awake, arise, spring forth.*

âwâcian, ôde, od (6), *to fail, decline, weaken.*

âweccan, ehte, cht (6), *to stir, awake, excite.*

âweorpan, wearp, worpen (1), *to cast aside, reject.*

awinnan, wan, wunnen (1), *to win, conquer.*

âwyrg(i)an, de, ed (6), *to curse, denounce.*

B.

Babi(y)lon, es, n. (irreg.), *Babylon.*

Babilonia, f.

Babilonige, adj., *Babylonian.*

bæðwa(e)g, es, 1, m., *a sea way, sea.*

bæl, es, 1, n., *a flame, burning.*

bælblŷs, e, 2, f., bælblŷse, an, 4, f., *a pile blaze, funereal fire.*

bælc, es, 1, m., *a covering, cloud, balcony.*

baêl, egesa, an, 4, m., *a terror of fire, great terror.*

bæman, de, ed (5), *to burn, to fire.*

balca, an, 4, m., *a covering.*

Baldazar, m. (irreg.), *Belshazzar.*

bân, es, 1, n., *a bone.*

bana, an, 4, m., *a slayer, murderer.*
G. banja.

bânhûs, es, 1, n., *a bone house, body.*

barenian, ôde, od (6), *to lay bare, expose.*

bâsnian, ede, ed (6), *to expect, await.*

basu (pl., wc), adj., *crimson, purple.*

be, prep., *by, at, of.* G. bi.

beâc(e)n, es, 1, n., *a beacon, sign, image.*

beadosearo (indic.), wes, 1, n., *war equipment, weapons.*

beadumægen, es, 1, n., *strength of battle, strength.*

beag, es, 1, m., *a jewel, treasure, garland* (bûgan).

b(e)ald, adj., *bold.* G. balþs.

bealde, adv., *boldly.*

bealo(w), es, 1, m., *woe, bale, evil.*

bealospel(l), es, 1, n., *an evil tale.*

bealusîð, es, 1, m., *a dire journey, adversity.*

beâm, es, 1, m., *a beam, pillar.* G. bagms.

bearhtm (byrhtm), es, 1, m., *a brightness, tumult, instant.*

bearm, es, 1, m., *a bosom.*

bearn, es, 1, n., *a son, child.* G. barn.

bearu, wes, 1, m., *a grove, wood.*

beâtan, beôt, beaten (5), *to beat, strike, hurt.*

bebeôdan, beâd, boden (3), *to order, enjoin.*

bebod, es, 1, n., *a decree, precept.*

bebûgan, beâh, bogen (3), *to enclose, surround.*

becuman (cwiman), com, (cwo(a)m), cumen (1), *to come, befall.*

befæðm(l)an, ede, ed (6), *to bound, embrace.*

befaran, fôr, faren (4), *to go round, encompass.*

befeolan, feal(h) (fæl), folen (1), *to fix in, to fasten.* M. 200.

beforan, prep., *before* (befeore).

begitan, geat, giten (ge(a)ten) (1), *to acquire, obtain.*

bego(a)ng, es, 1, m., *a course, circuit.*

behealdan, heôld, healden (5), *to behold, hold.*

behwylfan, ede, ed (6), *to subvert, overturn.*

belecgan, gde, gd (6), *to surround.*

belêgan, de (6), *to blaze, flame.*

bell, es, 1, m., *a cry, clamor.*

belûcan, leâc, locen (3), *to shut in, enclose.*

beme, an, 4, f., *a trumpet.*

ben(n), e, 2, f., *a prayer, entreaty.* G. bida.

bend, es, 1, m., *a band, bond.* G. bandi.

beôdan, beâd, boden (3), *to bid, order, proclaim.*

beôn, wæs, gewesen (irreg.), *to be.* G. wisan.

beorg(h), es, 1, m., *a mountain slope, citadel.*

beorhhlîð, es, 1, n., *a hill slope, summit.*

beorht, adj., *bright, lucid.* G. bairhts.

beorht, rodor, es, 1, m., *a bright firmament.* Beorht may be used as a suffix.

beorn, es, 1, m., *a chieftain, nobleman, man.* In poetry means a *man.*

beorsel(e), es, 1, m., e, 2, f., *a beerhall, hall.*

beôt, es, 1, n., *a threat, promise, peril.*

b(e)ôt, e, 2, f., *remedy, redress, amends* (to b(e)ote, *moreover*).

beô(t), hata, an, 4, m., *a promiser, surety, leader.*

beran, bær, boren (1), *to bear,
carry, observe.*

beréaflan (bereofan) (berofen),
ôde, od (6), *to bereave, deprive,
spoil.*

bereccan, re(a)hte, eht (6), *to relate.*

berênlan, ôde, od (6), *to kindle,
build a fire.*

berhtmhwat, adj., *quick, bright.*

berstan, bærst, borsten (1), *to
burst, scatter.*

beseôn, seah, sewen (1), *to look
about, observe.* G. gasaihwan.

besnædan, de, ed (6), *to cut, hew.*

bestêman, de, ed (6), *to besteam,
surround.*

beswælan, de, ed (6), *to burn,
singe.*

beswîcan, swâc, swicen (2), *to
entice, deceive.*

bêtan, te, ed (6), *to amend, restore.*

beþeccan, þeahte (þêhte), þeaht
(6), *to cover, conceal.*

bewindan, wand, wunden (1),
to wind, turn, circuit.

bewrecan, wræc, wrecen (1), *to
avenge, expel.*

bewrîgan, wrâh, wrîgen (2), *to
clothe, cover.*

bîdan, bâd, biden (2), *to await,
bide.* G. beidan.

biddan, bæd, beden (1), *to beg,
pray.* G. bidjan.

bifôn, fêng, fangen (5), *tó grasp,
hold, surround.*

bil(l), es, 1, n., *a sword, falchion.*

bi(y)le(y)(h)wit, adj., *merciful,
kind, innocent.*

bilswaðu, e, 2, f., *a sword track,
wound.*

bindan, band, bunden (1), *to
bind, restrain.*

biter, adj., *bitter, severe.* G. baitrs.

blâc, adj., *pale, shining.*

blæd, e, 2, f., *a branch, flower,
fruit, glory.*

blæst, es, 1, m., *a blast, wind.*

bland, es, 1, n., *a mingling, blending.*

blêd, e, 2, f., *a blade, branch.*

blestigan = bletsian. M. 20.

bletsian, ôde, od (6), *to bless, con-
secrate.*

blîð, adj., *blithe, happy.* G. bleiþs.

blîðe môd, *cheerful, happy-minded.*

blinnan, blan, blunnen (1), *to
cease, rest.*

blôd, es, 1, n., *blood, gore.* G. bloþ.

blôdegsa, an, 4, m., *a bloody terror,
storm.*

blôdig, adj., *bloody.*

bôc, e, 2, f. (irreg.), *a book, writing.*
G. boka.

bôcere, es, 1, m., *a writer, interpreter, wise man.*

bôcstæf, es, 1, m., *a letter, character.*

bôdi(ge)an, ôde, od (6), *to publish,
preach, order.*

bôg(h), es, 1, m., *a branch, bough.*

boga, an, 4, m., *a bow, arch, bending.*

bolgenmôd, adj., *angry, enraged.*

bord, es, 1, n., *a board, shield.* G.
baurd.

bordhréoða, an, 4, m., *a buckler.*

bôt(e), e, 2, f., an, 4, f., *a remedy,
amends.*

brâd, adj., *broad, ample.* G. braids.

bræd(d)an, de, ed (6), *to spread,
extend.*

bra(o)nd, es, 1, m., *a brand, torch.*

brecan, bræc, brecen (1), *to
break, violate.*

brego(u), m. (indec.), *a prince,
ruler.* Used in poetry as a prefix.

breman, de, ed (6), *to honor, cele-
brate.*

bre(y)me, adj., *notable, renowned.*

breost, e, 2, f., *a breast, bosom.* G.
brusts.

breóstgeþanc, es, 1, m., n., *inner thought*, thought, mind.

breóstloca, an, 4, m., a *breast-chamber*, recess of mind.

breóstnet, es, 1, n., a *breast-net*, shield.

bre(æ)sne, adj., *brazen*, mighty.

brim, es, 1, n., a *sea*, ocean. G. saiws.

brimfa(o)ru, e, 2, f., a *sea way*, ocean way.

bring, es, 1, m., an *offering*.

bringan, brang, brungen (1), *to bring*. G. briggan.

bringan, brohte, gebroht (6), *to bring*.

bróðorgyld, es, 1, n., *brother-vengeance*, vengeance.

brûn, adj., *brown*.

bryne, es, 1, m., a *burning heat*, a burning.

brytinan, ôde, od (6), *to dispense*, enjoy.

bryttian, ôde, od (6), *to divide*, distribute, enjoy.

bûan, de (6), *to dwell*, inhabit.

bufo(a)n, prep., *above*.

burh(g), e, 2, f., a *city* (beorgan). G. baurgs.

burhhleoð, es, 1, n., a *hill slope*, height.

burhsittend, es, 1, m. (part. noun), a *dweller*, inhabitant.

burhstede, es, 1, m., a *city place*, metropolis.

burhwaru, e, 2, f., a *city*, people.

burhweard, es, 1, m., a *city hold*, city ward.

butan(on), prep., conj., *but*, unless, without.

byrne, an, 4, f., a *trumpet*.

byrnan, barn, burnen (1), *to burn*. G. gabraunjan.

byrnende, part. adj., *burning*.

C.

cæg(e), e, 2, f., an, 4, f., a *key*.

Caldéas, â (pl.), *the Chaldeans*.

camp, es, 1, m., a *camp, field*, battle.

Canaanéas, ea (pl.), *the Canaanites*. M. 101.

carléas, adj., *careless*, reckless.

c(e)ald, es, 1, n., *cold*. G. kalds.

ceast(e)r, e, 2, f., a *city; castle*, town.

cempa, an, 4, m., a *warrior*, knight.

cêne, ôr, ôst, adj., *keen*, bold.

cennan, de, ed (6), *to beget*, produce.

ceorfan, cearf, corfen (1), *to carve*, hew.

ceósan, céâs, coren (3), *to choose, select*. G. kiusan.

cigean, cŷgde (6), *to call, name*, summon.

cinberg, es, 1, m., a *visor, chin-defence*.

clæne, adj., *clean;* adv., *entirely*.

clam(m), es, 1, m., *clay, a clamp*, band.

cneómæg, es, 1, m., a *kinsman*, relation.

cneóris(es), e, 2, f., a *family, tribe*, generation.

cneów, es, 1, n., a *knee, relationship*.

cneówsib(b), e, 2, f., a *race, relationship*.

cniht, es, 1, m., a *boy, youth*, attendant.

corðer, es, 1, n., a *company*, multitude, pomp.

cræft, es, 1, m., e, 2, f., *craft, skill*, power.

cringan, crang, crungen (1), *to cringe, submit*.

cûð, ôr, ôst, adj., *known, re-nowned.* G. kunþs.

cu(y)man, com, cumen (1), *to come.*

cumb(o)l, es, 1, n., *an ensign, image, standard.*

cunnan, cûðe, (ge)cûð (irreg.), *to know, be able.* G. kunnan.

cunnian, ôde, od (6), *to test, prove.*

cwal(u), e, 2, f., *a killing, death.*

cwe(a)lm, es, 1, n., *slaughter, death.*

cwên, e, 2, f., *a queen, woman, wife.*

cwiman, cwa(o)m, cumen (1), *to come.*

cwyld-rof, adj., *slaughter - re-nowned, brave.*

cŷðan, de(ðe), ed (6), *to declare, make known.* G. gakannjan.

cyme, es, 1, m., *a coming.*

cyme, adj., *fit, noble, comely.*

cyn, es, 1, n., *kin, race, tribe.*

cynegôd, adj., *nobly born, gentle.*

cynerîce, es, 1, n., *a realm, king-dom.*

cyneþrymm, es, 1, m., *a kingly host.*

cyning, es, 1, m., *a king, ruler.*

cyningdôm (cinedôm), es, 1, m., *a kingdom, power.*

cyr(r) (cerre), es, 1, m., *a turn, bending, return.*

cyrman, de (6), *to utter, cry out.*

cy(e)rran, de, ed (6), *to turn, change.*

cyst, e, 2, f., *choice, costliness, bounty.*

D.

daêd, e, 2, f., *a deed, an act* (dôn). G. gadeds.

dædhwat, adj., *active, bold.*

dædlêan, es, 1, n., *a reward, re-quital.*

dædweorc, es, 1, n., *a deed, feat, great work.*

dæg, es, 1, m., *a day.* G. dags.

dægsceado, es, 1, m., *a day-shade, shade.*

dægsce(y)ald, es, 1, m., *a day-shield, cloud.*

dægweorc, es, 1, n., *a day's work, stated service.*

dægwôma, an, 4, m., *the break of day, dawn.*

dælan, de, ed (6), *to deal, divide.* G. dailjan.

Daniel, m., *Daniel.*

David, es, m., *David.*

dêad, adj., *dead.* G. dauþs.

dêað, es, 1, m., *death* (pl. *spirits*).

dêaðdrepe, es, 1, m., *a death-blow, death.*

dêaðstede, es, 1, n., *a place of death, sepulchre.*

dêaw, es, 1, m., *the dew.*

dêaw-dr(l)êas, as, 1, m., *a dew-falling.*

dêawig, adj., *dewy.*

dêawigfeðer, e, 2, f., *a wing, a dewy feather.*

dêawigfeðere, adj., *dewy feath-ered, winged.*

dêma, an, 4, m., *a judge, ruler.*

dêman, de, ed (6), *to judge, deem.* G. domjan.

dêofol, es, 1, m., n., *the devil* (101 c).

dêofoldæd, e, 2, f., *devil-work, a wicked deed.*

dêofolgyld, es, 1, n., *an idol, idolatry.*

dêofolwitega, an, 4, m., *a false prophet, soothsayer.*

dêof, es, 1, m., *the deep, abyss.*

dêof, adj., *deep, great.* G. diups.

dêor, es, 1, n., *a wild beast, deer.* G. dius.

deor(e), adj., *dear, beloved* (dŷre).

déŏrmŏd, adj., *beloved, renowned.*

derian, ede, ed (6), *to harm, injure.*

Dira, n (irreg.), *Dura, Plain of Dura.*

dŏm, es, 1, m., *judgment, counsel, interpretation, power, law.*

dŏn, di(y)de, ge-dŏn (irreg.), *to do, execute.* G. taujan.

dréam, es, 1, m., *joy, gladness, music.*

dréamléas, adj., *sad, joyless.*

dréarung, e, 2, f., *a falling, distilling.*

drencflŏd, es, 1, n., *a deluge, flood.*

dréŏgan, dréah(g), drogen (3), *to bear, do, suffer.*

dréŏr, es, 1, m., *gore, blood.* Used as a prefix.

dreoran, drear (dreosan, dreas), droren (1), *to fall, perish.*

driht, e, 2, f., *a host, company, household.*

drihten, es, 1, m., *a lord, ruler, the Lord.* Used in composition.

drihtenweard, es, 1, m., *a guardian, master.*

drihtfolc, es, 1, n., *a multitude, the people.*

driht, ne, es, 1, m. (pl., drihtnéas, *carcasses*).

drysmian, de (6), *to obscure, darken.*

drofa, an, 4, m., *a drop, spot.*

druncen, adj., *drunken.*

drŷmust : see dŷre.

dugo(u)ð, e, 2, f., *rank, prosperity, people.*

dygle, adj., *secret* (digel); adv., *secretly* (dyglíce), *deeply.*

dŷre, ra, ost (drŷmust), adj., *dear, beloved.*

E.

éac, conj., *also, likewise.*

éaca, an, 4, m., *an addition, advantage.*

éacen, adj., *great, gifted* (éacan).

éad, adj., *rich, happy.*

éad, es, 1, n., *wealth, prosperity, joy.*

éadig, adj., *happy, blessed.*

éað(e), adj., *easy* (éaðor, ŏst); adv., *easily* (éð, éaðost).

éað(d)médu, pl. n., u, e, 2, f., *humility.*

éaðmédum, adv., *humbly.*

éaðmetto, f. (indec.), u, e, 2, f., *humility, submission.*

eafora, an, 4, m., *a son, descendant.*

éage, an, 4, n., *an eye.* M. 95. G. augo.

eald, adj., *old, ancient* (yldra, est).

ealdféond, es, 1, m., *an ancient foe.*

eal(l), adj., *all.*

(e)aldor, e, 2, f., *life.*

(e)aldor, es, 1, m., n., *a prince, ancestor, elder.*

ealdordŏm, es, 1, m., *eldership, power.*

ealdorlagu(e), e, 2, f. (leg, es, 1, m.), *destiny, life's decree.*

ealdorman, es, 1, m., *an alderman, ruler, one next to the king.*

ealdwérig, adj., *perverse, depraved.*

ealhstede, es, 1, m., *a hall-stead, palace.*

ealles, adv., *wholly, entirely.*

ear, es, 1, m., *the sea, ocean.*

earc, e, 2, f., *an ark, chest.* G. arka.

eard(ð), es, 1, m., *native soil, earth.*

earfoðmæecg, es, 1, m., a, an, 4, m., *an afflicted man, a sufferer.*

earfoðsíð, es, 1, m., *a hard jour-ney, a hard lot.*

earm, adj., *poor, wretched.* G. arms.

earmsceapen, adj., *ill-created, misshapen.*

earu, adj., *quick, swift, ready.*

éastréam, es, 1, m., *the sea, ocean.*

éast-weg, es, 1, m., *an east way, eastward.*

éce, adv., *always, eternal* (êc, also); adj., *perpetual.*

ecg, e, 2, f., *an edge, sword, war.*

edsceaft (sceaft), e, 2, f., *a new creation, regeneration.*

éð, adj., *mild, submissive.*

éðan (ýðan), de (6), *to overrun, devastate.*

éðel, es, 1, m., *home, native land, inheritance.*

éðelland, es, 1, n., *a native land, legacy.*

éðelléas, adj., *homeless, wretched.*

éðelriht, es, 1, n., *native right, land right.*

éðelweard, es, 1, m., *a native prince, people's guardian.*

éðfynde, adj., *easily found.*

efne, adv., *even, evenly, just, even as.*

efn-gedælan, de, ed (6), *to share evenly, divide.*

efn(i)an, (e)de, ed (6), *to do, exe-cute.*

eft-wyrd, adv., *afterward.*

ege-láfe, e, 2, f., *a fearful rem-nant, battle remnant.*

eg(e)le, adj., *troublesome, hateful.*

egesa, an, 4, m., *fear, terror.*

egesful(l), adj., *fearful, terrible.*

egeslíc, adj., *fearful, severe.*

egeslíce, adv., *fearfully, severely.*

egl(i)an, ede, ed (6), *to ail, trouble, torment.*

Egypte, e, f., *Egypt.*

Egypte, a, pl., *Egyptians.*

eht(i)an, ehte, ed (6), *to follow, harass.*

elpend, es, 1, m., *an elephant, walrus.*

elþéodig, adj., *foreign.*

ende, es, 1, m., *an end.* G. andeis (ands).

endedæg, es, 1, m., *a final day, the last day.*

endeléan, es, 1, n., *a final reward, punishment.*

enge, adj., *straight, narrow.*

engel, es, 1, m., *an angel, messen-ger.*

éode: see gán. G. gaggan.

eorð(e), e, 2, f., an, 4, f., *the earth, ground* (eardian).

eorðbuend, es, 1, m., *an earth-dweller, man.*

eorðcyn, es, 1, n., *the human race, men.*

eorðcyning, es, 1, m., *an earth-king, great king.*

eorðlíc, adj., *earthly.*

eorl, es, 1, m., *an earl, count.* This is a Danish word (yarl) transferred to English.

eorp, adj., *dark, dusky, wolf-colored.*

eorp (eorod), es, 1, m., *a host.*

éow: see þû.

éowian, de, ed (6), *to show, re-veal.*

esne (æsne), es, 1, m., *a servant, man.*

êst, es, 1, m., *favor, pleasure, grace.*

F.

fácen, es, 1, n., *fraud, guile, wickedness.*

fácne, adv., *evilly, deceitfully.*

fæc, es, 1, n., *a space, time, period.*

fæder, es (also indec. in sing.), 1, m., *father.* G. fader.

fæderäelo, f. (indec.), *ancestry, origin.*

fædercyn, es, 1, n., *a paternal race.*

fæðm, es, 1, m., *a fathom, grasp, embrace.* G. faþa.

fæge, adj., *dying, fated, accursed.*

fæg(e)r, adj., *fair, joyous.*

fægre, adv., *fairly, beautifully.*

fær, es, 1, m., *fear, danger, sudden coming.*

færbryne, es, 1, m., *sudden heat, great heat.*

færgryre, es, 1, m., *horror, dire terror.*

færspell, es, 1, n., *sudden tidings, alarm.*

færwundor, es, 1, n., *sudden wonder, great wonder.*

fæst, adj., *fast, firm, constant.*

fæstan, te (6), *to fast, expiate by fasting.*

fæste, adv., *fast, firmly.*

fæsten, es, 1, n., *a fastness, fortress.*

fæstlîc, adj., *fast, firm.*

fâh, adj., *hostile.*

fâmgian, ôde, od (6), *to foam, boil.*

fâming, adj., *foaming.*

fâmigbosm, es, 1, m., *a gulf, foamy bosom.*

fana, an, 4, m., *a flag, standard.*

fandian, ôde, od (6), *to try, test.*

faran, fôr, faren (4), *to go, march, die.* G. faran.

Faraon, es, m., *Pharaoh.*

fêa(w), adj. (indec.), *few* (dat., um). G. faws.

feax, es, 1, n., *hair.*

fêða, an, 4, m., *a foot-soldier, army, tribe.*

fêðe-gâst, es, 1, m., *a foot-guest, visitor, spirit of death.*

fela, adj. (indec.), *many, much.* G. fllu(s).

feld, es, 1, m., *a field, plain.*

feldhûs, es, 1, n., *a field-house, tent.*

feng, es, 1, m., *a grasp, hold.*

fêoh, os, 1, n. (irreg.), *cattle, money, property.* G. faihu.

fêohsceat, es, 1, m., *money, treasure.*

fêond, es, 1, m., *an enemy, fiend.*

fêor, adj., adv., *far.* G. fairra.

feorða, num. adj., *fourth.*

feor(h), es, 1, n., *soul, life, man.* G. fairhwus.

feorhgebeorh(g), es, 1, m., *life-security, safety.*

feorhlêan, es, 1, m., *a life-gift, reward.*

feorhnere, es, 1, m., *life, safety, salvation.*

fêran, de (6), *to journey, march, depart.*

fêr-clam, es, 1, m., *sudden fear.*

ferhð, es, 1, m., *life, mind, spirit.*

ferhðbana, an, 4, m., *a life-destroyer, murderer.*

ferhðloce, an, 4, m., *a life-enclosure, soul.*

ferian, (o)ede, ed (6), *to bear, carry.*

fîftig, num. adj., *fifty.*

findan, fand, funden (1), *to find, discover.*

fir, es, 1, m., *a living one, man.*

firen, adj., *sinful.*

fl(y)ren, e, 2, f., *a sin, crime.*

flân, e, 2, f., *a dart, arrow.*

flêam, es, 1, m., *flight, banishment.*

flêon, flêah, flogen (3), *to flee, escape* (flêogon). G. þliuhan.

flôd, es, 1, n., *a flood, wave.* G. flodus.

flôdblac, adj., *flood-pale, pale with fright.*

flôdeg(e)sa, an, 4, m., *flood-terror, fear.*

flôdweard, e, 2, f., *a flood-guardian.*

flôdweg, es, 1, m., *a flood-way, sea.*

flota, an, 4, m., *a ship, sailor.*

flŷs (flêôs), es, 1, n., *fleece, clothing.*

folc, es, 1, n., *folk, people.*

folccûð, adv., *popular, celebrated, well known.*

folcgesîð, es, 1, m., *a prince, ruler of the people.*

folcgetæl, e, 2, f., *the people, multitude.*

folcmægen, es, 1, n., *the people's force, the people.*

folcriht, es, 1, n., *folk-right, common privilege.*

folcsweot, es, 1, m., *a multitude, host.*

folctæl, e, 2, f., *a folk-list, genealogy.*

folctoga, an, 4, m.. *a folk-leader.*

folde, an, 4, f., *a field, the earth.*

folm(e), es, 1, m., an, 4, f., *a hand.*

for, prep., *for, before.* G. faur.

foran, adv., *before, only.*

forbærnan, de, ed (6), *to burn up, consume.*

forbrecan, bræc, brecen (1), *to destroy, break.*

forbyrnan, barn, burnen (1), *to burn, consume.*

forð, adv., *forth, thence.*

forðgang, es, 1, m., *a journey, progress.*

forðher(g)e, es, 1, m., *the van of an army.*

forðon, conj., *for, therefore.*

forðweg, es, 1, m., *a journey, onward way.*

foregenga, an, 4, m., *a herald, forerunner.*

foregengend, es, 1, m., *a forerunner.*

foremihtig, adj., *prepotent.*

foreweall, es, 1, m., *a forewall, rampart.*

foreweard, fyrra, adj., *fore.*

forfôn, fêng, fangen (5), *to seize, arrest.*

forgitan, geat (gæt), geten (1), *to forget, neglect.*

forgifan, geaf, gifen (1), *to forgive, give.*

forgyldan, geald, golden (1), *to pay, reward.*

forhabban, hæfde, ed (6), *to restrain, hold, deny.*

forht, adj., *timid, fearful.*

forhtian, ede, ed (6), *to fear, be alarmed.*

forl(a)êtan, lêt, l(a)êten (5), *to permit, forsake.*

forma (fruma), num, adj., super. of foreweard, *first, foremost.*

forniman, nam, numen (1), *to deprive, take away.*

forscûfan, scêaf, scofen (3), *to put aside, cast down.*

forst, es, 1, m., *frost.* G. frius.

forstandan, stôd, standen (4), *to withstand, protect, preside, understand.*

fracoð, adj., *vile, infamous.*

fræt(w)u, e, 2, f., *ornament, treasure.*

frêa, an, 4, m., *a lord, master* (præ). G. frauja.

frêaglêaw, adj., *prudent, very skilful.*

fr(e)ûsian, de (6), *to question, tempt.*

frêcne, adv., *boldly, fiercely;* adj., *bold.*

fremian, ede, ed (6), *to prosper, promote.*

fremman, de, ed (6), *to do, make, perpetrate.*

freó (indec.), f., *a ruler, mistress, woman* (freós).

freóbearn, es, 1, n., *noble children, free-born.*

freóbróðor, or (irreg.), m., *an own brother.*

freoðu(o), e, 2, f., *peace, blessing, liberty.*

freoðowær, e, 2, f., *a covenant, promise.*

freoh, adj., *free* (frî). G. freis.

freom, adj., *firm, strong.*

freomæg, es, 1, m., *a kinsman, relation.*

fretan, fræt, freten (1), *to eat, break.* G. fra-itan.

frið, es, 1, m., n., *peace, favor, protection.*

fri(g)nan, fræg, fru(g)nen (1), *to ask, learn by asking.*

fród, adj., *wise, prudent, old.*

frófer, e, 2, f., *solace, comfort.*

from, adj., *firm, good, bold.*

fruma(o), an, 4, m., *a beginning, origin* (on fruman, *at first*).

frumbearn, es, 1, n., *first-born.*

frumcneów, es, 1, n., *a progenitor, race.*

fru(o)mcyn, es, 1, n., *the origin of men, offspring.*

frumgár, es, 1, m., *a patriarch, chieftain.*

frumsceaft, e, 2, f., *first creation, a beginning.*

frumslæp, es, 1, m., *a first sleep.*

frumspræc, e, 2, f., *a first saying, promise.*

frymð, es, 1, m., *a beginning.*

fug(e)l, es, 1, m., *a fowl, bird.*

ful, adj., *foul.* G. fuls.

ful(l), adj., *full, perfect.* G. fulls.

furðor, adv., *forth,* comp. of forð.

fûs, adj., *ready, quick.*

fyll, e, 2, f., es, 1, m., *ruin, slaughter, fall.*

fyllan, de, ed (6), *to finish, fulfil.*

fyr, es, 1, n., *fire.*

fyrd, e, 2, f., *an army, expedition.*

fyrdgetrum, es, 1, n., *a martial band, host.*

fyrdleóð, es, 1, n., *a war song.*

fyrdwîc, es, 1, n., *a camp, army station.*

fyren, adj., *fiery.*

fyrendæd, e, 2, f., *an evil deed, sin.*

fyrmest: see foreweard.

fyrndæg, es, 1, m., *yore, olden time, days of yore.*

fyrst, e, 2, f., *a space, delay.*

fyrstmearc, e, 2, f., *a space, period.*

G.

gâd (gæd), es, 1, n., *want, need.*

gædeling, es, 1, m., *a comrade, associate.*

gærs: see græs.

galen, gôl, galen (4), *to sing.*

gam(e)ol, adj., *old, hoary.*

gân (gegân), éode, gegân (irreg.), *to go, to go through, practise.*

gang, es, 1, m., *a way, journey, march.*

gangan, gêng, (geóng) (5) (irreg.), *to go.*

gâr, es, 1, m., *a spear, javelin.*

gârbeám, es, 1, m., *a spear-beam, sword-handle.*

gârberend, es, 1, m., *a spear-bearing one, warrior.*

gârfaru, e, 2, f., *a martial way.*

gârhéaf, es, 1, m., *an army band, army.*

gârsecg, es, 1, m., *the sea, ocean.*

gârwudu, â, 3, m., *spear-wood, a spear, beam.*

gâ(e)st, es, 1, m., *a ghost, spirit.*

gê: see þû, *ye.* G. jus, izwis.

geálhmôd, adj., *sad-minded, gloomy.*

geare (gêre), adv., *well.*

gearu (gearwe), adj., adv., *ready* (gearo).

gebædan, de, ed (6), *to persuade, compel.*

gebéodan, béad, boden (3), *to order, enjoin.*

gebeorgan, bearh, borgen (1), *to save, defend.*

gebidan, bâd, biden (2), *to abide, await.*

gebindan, band, bunden (1), *to bind.*

geblendan, bland, blonden (1), *to mix, corrupt.* G. blaudan.

gebletsig(i)an, ôde, od (6), *to bless.*

gebycgan, bohte, boht (6), *to buy, secure.*

gecéosan, céas, coren (3), *to choose, select.*

gecweðan, cwæð, cweden (1), *to say, declare.*

gecyðan, ôde, ed (6), *to make known, manifest, tell.*

gecynde, adj., *natural, genial.*

gedælan, de, ed (6), *to divide, distribute.*

gedêman, de, ed (6), *to judge, decree.*

gedôn, di(y)de, dôn (6) (irreg.), *to do, act.*

gedrencan, te, ed (6), *to submerge, drown.*

gedréosan, dréas, droren (3), *to fall together, to rush, overthrow.*

gedriht, e, 2, f., *a host, company.*

gedrŷm(e) (gedrême), adj., *joyous, cheerful.*

gedwola, an, 4, m., *an error, deceit; one in error.*

geeglan, de, ed (6), *to injure, afflict.*

gefaran, fôr, faren (4), *to proceed, depart.*

gefeallan, féol, feallen (5), *to fall, deluge.*

geféon (feohan), feah, fegen (1), *to rejoice, exult.*

geféran, de, ed (6), *to go, journey.*

gefeterian, ôde, od (6), *to fetter, bind.*

gefihan, feah, fehen (1), *to rejoice, be glad.*

gefiŷman, de, ed (6), *to banish, expel.*

gefræge, es, 1, n., *an inquiry, asking.*

gefræge, adj., *known, famous, notorious.*

gefrécnian, ôde, od (6), *to corrupt, make evil.*

gefremman, de, ed (6), *to do, work.*

gefri(g)nan, fra(eg)(n), fru(g)-nen (1), *to ask, learn by asking.*

gefyllan, de, ed (6), *to fell, cut down.*

gefyllan, de, ed (6), *to accomplish, fulfil.*

gefŷsan, de, ed (6), *to hasten.*

geglêdan, de, ed (6), *to kindle, lighten.*

gegnunga, adv., *immediately.*

gegrind, es, 1, n., *a crash, grinding.*

gehâtan, hêt, haten (5), *to promise, vow.*

gehealdan, héold, healden (5), *to hold, possess.* G. haldan.

gehladan, hlôd, hla(e)den (4), to load, heap, burden.

ge(h)uipan, (h)nâp, (h)nipen (2), to arise as a cloud, to cloud.

gehwâ, es, adj. pro., whoever, each one, every.

gehweorfan, hwearf, hworfen (1), to turn, change, return.

gehwilc, adj. pro., each, every.

gehy(c)gan, de, ed (6), to consider, devise.

gehygd, es, 1, m., e, 2, f., thought, mind, reflection.

gehyld, es, 1, n., guardianship, custody.

gehŷran, de (6), to hear, obey.

gelâd, es, 1, m., a way, course.

gelaǒ, adj., hostile.

gelæd(d)an (gelêdan), de, ed (6), to lead, bring.

gelæstan, te, ed (6), to do, perform.

geléafa, an, 4, m., faith, assent.

gelîc, adj., like, similar. G. galeiks.

gelimpan, lamp, lumpeŋ (1), to happen, befall.

gelŷfan, de, ed (6), to concede, grant, believe.

gemæne, adj., common, general.

gemættan, te, ed (od) (6), to dream.

gemet, adj., meet, fit.

gemengan, de, ed (6), to mingle, defile, confuse.

gemunan, de (6), to remember.

gemynd, es, 1, n., e, 2, f., thought, mind, consideration.

gemyndg(1)an, de, ed (6), to be mindful, remember.

gemyndig, adj., mindful.

gemyntan, te, ed (6), to resolve, purpose.

genægan, de, ed (6), to assail, afflict, subdue.

genâpan, nêǒp, napen (5), to overwhelm, destroy.

geneǒian, de, ed (6), to venture, dare, press.

gneerian, ede, ed (6), to save, preserve.

gengan, de (6), to go.

geng (geong), adj., young.

geniman, nam, numen (1), to take, obtain.

geniwian, ôde, od (6), to revive, renew.

genŷdan, de (6), to compel, force.

geǒc, e, 2, f., aid, comfort.

geǒcian, ôde, od (6), to save, help, strengthen.

geǒcor, ôst, adj., sad, painful.

geǒcre, adv., severely.

geofon, es, 1, n., the sea, deep.

geǒguǒ, e, 2, f., youth. G. junda.

geǒmra, adj., grim, sad.

geond. prep., adv., beyond, through, among.

geondsâwan, seǒw, sâwen (5), to scatter, sow abroad.

georn, adj., willing, anxious, zealous.

georne, adv., willingly, earnestly.

georulîce, adv., zealously.

gerædu, e, 2, f., trappings, harness.

gerec(e)mian, ôde, od (6), to explain, reckon.

gerêfa, an, 4, m., a companion, associate.

geregnian, ôde (6), to arrange, set in order.

geriman, de, ed (6), to count, compute.

geri(y)snc, adj., proper, convenient; es, 1, n., convenience, propriety.

gerum, adj., great, spacious.

Gerusalem, f. (irreg.), Jerusalem.

gerŷman, de, ed (6), *to enlarge; open, lay waste.*

gerŷne, es, 1, n., *a mystery, decree.*

gesælan, de, ed (6), *to bind.*

gesamnian, ôde, od (6), *to gather, assemble.*

gesceadan, scéod, scaden (5), *to divide, separate.*

gesceaðan, scéod, sceaðen (5), *to injure, overwhelm.*

gesceaft, e, 2, f., *a decree.*

gescéon, ôde (6), *to appoint, befall.*

gescrîfan, scrâf, scrifen (2), *to impose, prescribe.*

gescy(i)dan, de, ed (6), *to shield, protect.*

gescyldan, de, ed (6), *to shield, guard.*

gesecgan, sægde, sægd (6), *to declare, explain, confess.*

geseðan, de, ed (6), *to affirm, verify.*

gesettan, te, t (6), *to set, settle, place.*

geséon (seohan), seah, sewen (1), *to see, observe.*

gesîð, es, 1, m., *a companion, associate.*

gesigefæst, adj., *triumphant, victorious.*

gesî(y)ne, adj., *manifest, visible.*

gesittan, sæt, seten (1), *to sit, dwell.*

gesleân, slôh(g), slegen (4), *to strike, slay, kill.*

gespannan, spên (éon), spannen (5), *to join, span.*

gestandan, stôd, standen (4), *to stand.* G. gastandan.

gestêpan, te (6), *to raise, erect.*

gestîgan, stâh, stigen (2), *to rise, ascend.*

gestillan, de, ed (6), *to stay, restrain.*

gestréon, es, 1, n., *gain, treasure.*

gestrûdan, stréad, stroden (3), *to plunder, ravage.*

geswelgan, swealh(g), swolgen (1), *to swallow, devour.*

gesweorcan, swéarc, sworcen (3), *to darken, obscure.*

geswêðan, de, ed (6), *to confirm, strengthen.*

gesy(i)hð, e, 2, f., *a sight, view.*

gesyllan, sealde, seald (6), *to give, deliver.*

gesynt(o), e, 2, f., *fruit, prosperity.*

getellan, tealde, teald (6), *to count, number.*

getenge, adj., *heavy, oppressive.*

getéon, téah(g), togen (3), *to draw, educate.*

getéon, de (6), *to design, appoint, frame.*

geþanc, es, 1, m., n., *mind, thought.*

geþencan, þohte, þoht (6), *to think, devise.*

geþéon, þâh, þogen (2), *to thrive, flourish.*

geþing, es, 1, n., *a council, assembly.*

geþoht, es, 1, m., *a thought, resolve.* G. þuhtus.

getîðian, ôde, od (ad) (6), *to grant, perform.*

getimbrian, ôde, od (6), *to build, erect.* G. gatimrjan.

getwæfan, de, ed (6), *to divide, divert, distract.*

gewadan, wôd, waden (4), *to wade through, pervade.*

gewealc, es, 1, n., *a rolling, an attack.*

geweald, e, 2, f., *power, rule.*

geweaxan, w(e)ôx, weaxen (4), *to grow, increase.* G. wahsjan.

gewemman, de, ed (6), *to stain, defile.*

geweorðan, wearð, worden (1), *to happen, occur.*

geweorðian, ôde, od (6) *to honor, adorn.*

gewindæg, es, 1, m., *a day of sorrow, humiliation.*

gewindan, wand, wunden (1), *to wind about, circle, enrol.*

gewita, an, 4, m., *a sage, witness, comrade.*

gewitan, wât, witen (2), *to depart, die.*

gewit(t), es, 1, n., *mind, knowledge, skill.*

gewrit, es, 1, n., *a writing, Scripture.*

gewun, adj., *wont, accustomed.*

gewu(y)rðian, ôde, od (6), *to adorn, magnify.*

gewyrcan, worhte, worht (6), *to work, effect.*

gewyrht, es, 1, n., *a deed, desert.*

gewyrhto (indec.), *deserts, merits.*

gif, conj., *if, though.* G. ibai.

gifan, geaf (gæf), gifen (1), *to give, bestow.*

gifu, e, 2, f., *a gift, favor.*

gihðu (gehðu), e, 2, f., *spirit, mind, anxiety.*

gi(y)ld, es, 1, n., *a payment, offering, idol.*

gi(y)lp, es, 1, m., *glory, boasting.*

gilpan, gealp, golpen (1), *to boast, vaunt.*

gîn, es, 1, n., *an expanse, opening.*

ginfæst, adj., *ample, vast.*

ging, ra, ost, adj., *young.* G. juggs.

glade, adv., *gladly, willingly.*

glâde, es, 1, m., *a fall, setting (of the sun).*

glæd, adj., *glad.* G. hlas.

glædmôd, adj., *glad, glad-minded.*

gléàw, adj., *wise, skilful, clever.*

gléàwmôd, adj., *prudent, prudent-minded.*

glêd, e, 2, f., *a coal, fire.*

gnorne, adj., *sad, mournful.*

gôd, adj., *good.* G. gods.

god, es, 1, m., *God* (pl., m., n., *idols, gods*). G. Guþa.

godsæd, es, 1, n., *a godly race, seed.*

godspellian, ôde, od (6), *to gospel, preach.*

gold, es, 1, n., *gold.* G. gulþ.

goldfæt, es, 1, n., *a gold vessel, costly vessel.*

goldhord (heord), es, 1, m., *a treasure, treasury.*

goldweb, es, 1, n., *purple, tapestry.*

grædig, adj., *greedy.* G. gredags.

græs, es, 1, n., *grass.* G. gras.

gr(a)etan, grêt, gr(a)eten (5), *to weep, lament.*

gra(o)m, adj., *fierce, angry.*

gramlîce, adv., *fiercely.*

grên, adj., *green.*

grêtan, te, ed (6), *to greet, approach.*

grim, adj., *severe.*

grimhelm, es, 1, m., *a grim visor, masked helmet.*

grimme, adv., *sternly.*

grindan, grand, grunden (1), *to grind, crush.*

grome, adv., *fiercely.*

grund, es, 1, m., *ground, earth.* G. grundus.

grymetan, ôde, od (6), *to clash, raze.*

gryre, es, 1, m., *a dread, terror.*

gûð, e, 2, f, *battle, war.* Used as a prefix.

gûðcyst, e, 2, f., *a war tribe.*

gûðfremmend, es, 1, m., *a war-worker, warrior.*

gûð-myrc (mearc), e, 2, f., *a hostile frontier.*

Gûðmyrce, pl., *the Ethiopians.*

gûðþreat, es, 1, m., *a war-host, host.*

gûðweard, es, 1, m., *a war-guard, protector.*

guma, an, 4, m., *a groom, man* (gŷmau).

gumrîce, es, 1, n., *a realm, high kingdom.* gum, as a prefix, denotes excellence.

gy(i)ddig(e)an, ede, ed (6), *to be giddy, dazzled, troubled.*

gyldan, geald, golden (1), *to pay, requite, sacrifice.*

gylden, adj., *golden.* G. gulþcins.

gyllan, ede (6), *to roar, yell, cry.*

gylpplega, an, 4, m., *a boastful play, conflict, battle.*

gŷman, de (6), *to regard, observe, protect.*

gyrdwîte, es, 1, n., *a rod of punishment, a rod.*

gystsel(e), es, 1, m., e, 2, f., *a guest-hall.*

gyt, conj., *yet.*

H.

habban, hæfde, ed(d), irreg., *to have, reckon.* G. haban.

hâd, es, 1, m., *form, condition, habit.* (Eng. hood.)

hæð, e, 2, f., *a heath.* G. haiþl.

hæðen, adj., *heathen, pagan.*

hæðen, es, 1, m., *a pagan, heathen.*

hæðencyning, es, 1, m., *a pagan king.*

hæðengyld, es, 1, n., *an idol, heathen image.*

hæft, es, 1, n., *a haft, handle, captivity;* es, 1, m., *a captive.*

hægsteald (heahsteald), es, 1, m., *one of high degree, a bachelor, leader.*

hæleð, es, 1, m., *a hero, man.*

hæs, e, 2, f., *a command, behest.* G. haiti.

hæto (iudec.), f., *heat.*

hætu, e, 2, f., *heat.*

hæwen, adj., *blue, azure.*

hâl, adj., *hale, safe, healthy.* G. halls.

hâ(e)lig, adj., *holy.*

hâlswurðung, e, 2, f., *supplication, entreaty.*

hâm, es, 1, m., *a home, home.* G. haims.

hâmsittend, adj., *home-sitting, abiding.*

hand, â(e), 3, f., *a hand.* G. handus.

handléan, es, 1, n., *a reward, recompense.*

handplega, an, 4, m., *hand-play, encounter.*

handrôf, adj., *famed of hand, famous.*

hâr, adj., *hoary, gray.*

hâso, adj., *livid, rough.*

hât, adj., *hot.*

hât, es, 1, m., n., *heat.*

hât = gehât, 1, n., *a promise.*

hâtan, hêt (hêht), hâten (5), *to command;* pass., hâtte, *called, named.*

hâtwende, adj., *heated, torrid.*

hê, pro., *he.* Used also indefinitely, *they.*

heaðorinc, es, 1, m., *a war-man, hero.*

heaðowylm, es, 1, m., *a battle-wave, deadly feud.*

heaf, es, 1, m., *a wailing, mourning.*

heá(h), hŷrra, hŷhst (heáhst), adj., *high.* G. hauhs.

héahcyning, es, 1, m., *a high king, lord.*

héahfæder, es, 1, m. (also indec.), *a high father, patriarch.*

héahheort, adj., *proud, high-minded.*

héahla(o)nd, es, 1, n., *a high land.*

héahst : see heah.

héahtréow, e, 2, f., *a high compact, solemn league.*

héahþegnung, e, 2, f., *high service, duty.*

héahþungen, adj., *noble, high-born.*

healdan, héold, healden (5), *to hold, observe.*

healf, e, 2, f., *a half, side, part.* G. halba.

heall, e, 2, f., *a hall, house.*

héap, es, 1, m., *a heap, troop, phalanx.*

heard, adj., *hard, severe, bold.* G. hardus.

hearde, adv., *dearly, severely.*

hearg, e, 2, f., *an idol.*

he(a)rh(g), es, 1, m., *an idol, altar, grove, heathen temple.*

hearm, es, 1, m., *harm, hurt.*

he(a)rra, an, 4, m., *a lord, master.*

héaseld, es, 1, n., *a high seat, throne.*

hebban, hôf, hafen (4), *to heave, raise, exalt.*

Hebréos : see Ebréos.

hédan, de (6), *to heed, regard.*

héhþegen, es, 1, m., *a chief servant, attendant.*

hell, e, 2, f., *hell, the grave.* G. halja.

helm, es, 1, m., *a cover, helmet, chieftain.*

help, e, 2, f., *help, aid.*

helpan, healp, holpen (1), *to help, assist.* G. hilpan.

helpend, es, 1, m., *a helper.*

heofon, es, 1, m., heofone, an, 4, f., *heaven.* G. himins.

heofon (irreg.), e, 2, f., *lamentation, mourning.*

heofonbeacen, es, 1, n., *a heavenly sign, beacon.*

heofonbeorht, adj., *heaven-bright, glorious.*

heofoncandel, es, 1, n., *a heavenly light, the sun.*

heofoncol, es, 1, n., *a heavenly coal, heat of the sun.*

heofoncyning, es, 1, m., *heaven's King.*

he(o)fonfugo(e)l, es, 1, m., *the fowl of heaven.*

heofonheah, adj., *lofty, heaven-high.*

heofonrîce, es, 1, n., *a heavenly kingdom, kingdom of heaven.*

heofonsteorra, an, 4, m., *a star of heaven.*

heofontungel, es, 1, m., n., *a star of heaven, the sun.*

héold, e, 2, f., *a lair, cave, hold.*

heolfer, es, 1, n., *gore, blood.*

heolsto(e)r, es, 1, n., *a cover, darkness.*

heonan, adv., *hence.*

heorofæðm, es, 1, m., *a warlike grasp, arms.*

heor(o)t, es, 1, m., *a hart, stag.*

heorowulf, es, 1, m., *an army-wolf, a warrior.*

heorte, an, 4, f., *the heart.* G. hairto.

heorugrim, adj., *sword-cruel, savage.*

héran (hergan), de, ed (6), *to praise, honor.*

here, (g)es, 1, m., *an army, a host.* G. harjis.

herebléað, adj., *army-fearful, panic-stricken.*

herebyme, an, 4, f., *a war-trum-pet.*

hereclst, e, 2, f., *a choice host, warlike band.*

herefugol, es, 1, m., *a war-fowl, raven.*

herepað (pæð), es, 1, m., n., *an army-path, military way.*

hererĕáf, es, 1, n., *spoil, army-clothing.*

herestrǣt, e, 2, f., *an army-way, a road.*

heretŷma, an, 4, m., *leader of a host, a leader.*

herepreat, es, 1, m., *a company, army, formidable post.*

herewîsa, an, 4, m., *an army-leader, commander.*

herewŏp, es, 1, m., *an army-cry.*

herewŏsa, an, 4, m., *a hostile band.*

her(g)e, es, 1, m., *an army, expedition* (herige).

heri(ge)an, ede, ed (6), *to praise, laud.*

hete, es, 1, m., *hate, envy.*

hettan, te (6), *to drive, pursue.*

hettend, es, 1, m., *a pursuer, an enemy.*

Hierusalem, e, f., *Jerusalem.*

hi(y)gecræft, es, 1, m., e, 2, f., *mental skill, power of thought.*

hi(y)geþancol, adj., *mindful, thoughtful.*

hiht, e, 2, f., *hope.*

hild, e, 2, f., *a battle, war.* Used as a prefix.

hi(y)ld, es, 1, m., *protection, favor.*

hildecalla, an, 4, m., *a man of war, a hero.*

hildespell, es, 1, n., *a war-speech, harangue.*

hindan, adv., *from behind.*

hleahtorsmlð, es, 1, m., *a laughter-smith, a laugher.*

hlenca, an, 4, m., e, an, 4, f., *a chain.*

hleo(w), es, 1, m., *a shade, protection.*

hleŏðor, es, 1, m., *a sound, voice, revelation.*

hleŏðorcwy(i)de, es, 1, m., *a revelation, prophecy.*

hleŏðrian, ŏde, od (6), *to sound, sing, prophesy.*

hlifian, ŏde, od (6), *to raise, rise, tower.*

hlud, adj., *loud.*

hlu(t)tor, adj., *clear, bright.*

hlŷ(i)gan, hlâh(g), hligen (2), *to call upon, summon.*

hlŷp, es, 1, m., *a leap, jump.*

hlŷst, e, 2, f., *a listening, hearing.*

hnîgan, hnâh(g), hnigen (2), *to bow, bow down, incline.*

hogian, ŏde, od (6), *to think, study.*

hold, adj., *true, kind, friendly.* G. hulþs.

holm, es, 1, m., *a sea, an abyss.*

holmeg, adj., *wet, stormy.*

holmweall, es, 1, m., *a sea-wall, dike.*

holt, es, 1, n., *a grove, wood.*

hordmægen, es, 1, n., *a treasure-house.*

hordweard, es, 1, m., *a treasure-ward, guardian of treasure.*

horn, es, 1, m., *a horn, trumpet.* G. haurn.

horse, adj., *wise, prudent.*

hrǎðe, adv., *quickly.*

hræfn, es, 1, m., *a raven, the Danish standard.*

hrægl, es, 1, m., *clothing, a garment.*

hræw (hreaw), es, 1, m., *a carcass.*

hream, es, 1, m., *a din, noise.*

hreddan, de, ed (G), *to rescue,
deliver.*

hrê̌ð, adj., *stern, savage.*

hrê̌ðan, de (G), *to excite, cheer.*

hrê̌ðer, es, 1, m., *the mind,
breast.*

hrê̌ðergleaw, adj., *prudent, saga-
cious.*

hrêm(m)an, de, ed (G), *to hinder,
disquiet.*

hrê̌ohmôd, adj., *fierce, fierce-
minded;* es, 1, n., *fierceness.*

hrêpan (hrôpan), hr(ê)op, hrê-
pen (5), *to call, scream.*

hrôf, es, 1, m., *a roof, top.*

hruse, an, 4, f., *a rock, hill.*

hryre, es, 1, m., *ruin, a falling.*

hû, adv., *how.* G. hwaiwa.

hû̌ð, e, 2, f., *prey, spoil, booty.*

huslfæt, es, 1, n., *a vessel of sacrifice* (housel).

hwâ, interrog. pro., *who;* also
as a relative. G. hwas.

hwæ̌ð(e)re, conj., *yet, whether.*

hwæl, es, 1, m., *a whale.*

(h)wæl, es, 1, n., *slaughter.*

hwæl, es, 1, m., *a wheel, circuit.*

hwæt, interj., *lo! behold!*

hwê̌op (wôp), es, 1, m., *a whoop,
cry.*

hw(y)(v)eorfan, hwearf, hworfen (1), *to turn, change, pass.*

hwîl, e, 2, f., *a while, time.*

hwî(y)lc, adj. pro., *which, of
what kind.* G. hwi-leiks.

hwile, an, 4, f., *a while, period.*
G. hweila.

hwîlum(on), adv., *once, some-
time, a while.*

hwît, adj., *white.* G. hweits.

hwonne, adv., *when.*

hwôpan, hwê̌op, hwepen (5), *to
cry, call, threaten.*

hwyrft, es, 1, m., *a space, circuit*

hycgan (hoglan), Ode, od (G), *to
think, meditate.*

hyge (hige), es, 1, m., *mind,
thought, anxiety.*

hyl(l), es, 1, m., *a hill, mountain.*

hyld(o), e, 2, f., *love, favor.*

hynð̌u, e, 2, f., *injury, insult, dis-
grace;* hynð̌o, indec.

hŷran, de, ed (G), *to hear, obey.*

hyrde, es, 1, m., *a guardian.*

hysc (hyss), es, 1, m., *a youth,
male.*

I (J).

Iacob (Jacob), es, m., *Jacob.*

ic, pro., *I.*

îcan: see ŷcan.

in, prep., *in, into.*

inca for incer: see þû, *your, of
you.* G. iggkwar.

inca, an, 4, m., *doubt.*

inca-þê̌od, e, 2, f., *folk-unity,
union.* Used adverbially, *in
union.*

ing (geong), adj., *young.*

in-gefolc, es, 1, n., *people, inhabitants.*

ingemen, adv., *in common.*

ingere, adv., *formerly.*

ingeþanc, es, 1, m., *inward
thought, thought.*

in-geþê̌od, e, 2, f., *people, nation.*

inlende, adj., *inland, domestic.*

innan, prep., *in, within.*

Joseph, es, m., *Joseph.*

Isaac, es, m., *Isaac.*

îsen (îren), es, 1, n., *iron.* G.
eisarn.

îsernher(g)e, es, 1, m., n., *an
iron host.*

Isra(h)êl, es, m., *Israel.*

Judas, as (irreg.), *Judah.*

Judêas, â, m. (pl.), *the Jews.*

Iudisc (Judisc), adj., *Judaish, of the tribe of Judah.*

Iu-gêre (geára), adv., *formerly.*

L.

lâcan, lêc, la(e)cen (5), *to play, wave, sacrifice.*

lâð, adj., *hateful, evil, troublesome.*

lâð, es, 1, n., *evil, harm, enmity.*

lâðsearo, es, 1, n., *a hateful device, weapon.*

lâðsîð (ladsîð), es, 1, m., *a dire journey.*

lædan, de, ed (6), *to lead, guide.* G. galeiþan.

læne, adj., *frail, slender.*

lærig, es, 1, m., *a rim of a shield, a shield.*

læstan, te (6), *to follow, observe, execute.*

lætan (lêtan), lêt, luêten (5), *to let, permit.*

lagu, â, 3, f., *water.*

laguland, es, 1, n., *water-deluged land.*

lagu(o)streâm, es, 1, m., *a stream, water-stream.*

land, es, 1, n., *land.* G. land.

landgesceaft, e, 2, f., *a creation, people.*

landman, es, 1, m., *a landman, native.*

landriht, es, 1, n., *a land-right, common right.*

lâf, e, 2, f., *a remnant.*

lang, leng(ra), adj., *long.* G. laggs.

lange, adv., *long, a long time.*

langsum, adj., *lasting, longsome, slow.*

langung, e, 2, f., *a longing, desire.*

lâr, e, 2, f., *lore, learning, command.*

lâst, es, 1, m., *a trace, footstep.*

lâstweard, es, 1, m., *a successor;* adv., *toward the last.*

lât(þ)eow, es, 1, m., *a guide, leader.*

leán, es, 1, n., *a reward, price.*

leás, adj., *less, wanting.* G. laus.

lengian, de, ed (6), *to prolong, slight.*

leód, es, 1, m., *a ruler, prince of the people.*

leód, e, 2, f., *the people.*

leódfruma, an, 4, m., *a patriarch, leader.*

leódhata, an, 4, m., *a tyrant, hater of the people.*

leódmægen, es, 1, n., *the people's force, valor.*

leódscearu, e, 2, f., *a region, nation.*

leódscipe, es, 1, m., *a people, nation.*

leódweard, es, 1, m., *a guardian of men, leader.*

leódwere (weras), nom. pl., *the people.*

leódwerod, es, 1, n., *a host, a nation.*

leóf, adj., *dear, beloved.*

leófan, leáf, lofen (3), *to choose, enjoy, prefer.*

leógan, leáh(g), logen (3), *to deceive, lie, betray.*

leoht, es, 1, n., *light.* G. liuhaþ.

leoht, adj., *light, clear.*

leohtfruma, an, 4, m., *source of light, God.*

leóma, an, 4, m., *a ray, beam of light.*

leon, es, 1, m., f. (irreg.), (leo, on), *a lion.*

leornian(igan), ôde, od (6), *to learn, acquire.*

lîc, es, 1, n., *a body, form.*

licgan, læg, legen (1), *to lie down (to die)*.

licwund, e, 2, f., *a body-wound, sore*.

lif, es, 1, n., *life*. G. libains.

lifdæg, es, 1, m., *life's day, a lifetime*.

liffréa, an, 4, m., *lord of life, a master*.

liffrumᴀ, an, 4, m., *author of life, Lord*.

lifi(g)an, leofôde (lŷfode) (6), *to live* (lifg(e)an).

lifigend, part. adj., *living*.

lif(t)weg, es, 1, m., *a life-way, way of life*.

lig(g), es, 1, n., *a flame, fire*.

lige, es, 1, m.,

liget, es, 1, n., *lightening, a flame, fire*.

ligfŷr, es, 1, n., *a fire-flame, fire*.

lind, e, 2, f., *a shield, linden*.

linde, an, 4, f.,

linnan, lan, lunnen (1), *to cease, part from*.

liss, e, 2, f., *grace, favor*.

lixan, te (6), *to shine, glitter*.

loce, es, 1, m., *a lock of hair, hair*.

lôclan, ôde, od (6), *to look, see*.

lôf, es, 1, m., n., *praise*.

lofian, ôde, od (6), *to laud, praise*.

lufe, an, 4, f., *love, favor*. G. lubo.

lufen, e, 2, f., *love, desire, expectation*.

lufian, ôde, od (6), *to love, cherish*.

lust, es, 1, m., *desire, delight*. G. lustus.

ly(i)bban, lifde (6), *to live*.

lyft, e, 2, f., *air, cloud*.

lyft-edor, es, 1, m., *aerial dwellings*.

lyfthelm, es, 1, m., *an air-cover, cloud*.

lyftlaêend, part. adj., *sporting in air*.

lyftwundor, es, 1, n., *an air-wonder, miracle*.

ly(i)geword, es, 1, n., *a false word, falsehood*.

ly(i)gnian, ede, ed (6), *to deny, falsify*.

lŷ(i)htan, te (6), *to shine, dawn*.

lyst, e, 2, f., *desire, love*.

lyt, es, 1, n., *a little*.

lyt, adv., *little*. G. leitils.

lyt(e)l, num. adj., *little*.

M.

mâ. See micel. G. mais.

mad(ð)m, es, 1, m., *treasure, a gift; vessel*.

mâð(w)mhord, es, 1, n., *treasure*.

mæcg, es, 1, m., *a son, youth*.

mæg, es, 1, m., *a kinsman*.

mægburh, e(ge), 2, f., *kinsfolk, family*.

mægen, es, 1, n., *force, power*.

mægenscipe, es, 1, m., *supremacy*.

mægenrôf, adj., *renowned in might, mighty*.

mægenþreat, es, 1, m., *a mighty band, army*.

mægenþrym, es, 1, m., *power, dignity*.

mægenwisa, an, 4, m., *a great leader, chieftain*.

mægwine, es, 1, m., *a kinsman, friend*.

mæl, es, 1, n., *a meal, repast*. G. mel.

mæl-mête, es, 1, m., *food, meal-meat*.

m(a)ere, adj., *great, more* (mêre).

mære-torht, adj., *very bright, clear-shining.*

mæst-râp, es, 1, m., *a mast-rope.*

mætan, te, od (6), *to dream.*

mæte, adj. (ra, ost), *even, moderate.*

mæting, e, 2, f., *a dream, dreaming.*

maga, an, 4, m., *a son, kinsman.*

magan, meahte (mihte) (irreg.), *may, can, to be able.*

magoræswa, an, 4, m., *a leader, kindred chief.*

man, es, 1, m. (irreg.), *man.* G. manna.

mân, es, 1, n., *sin, evil.*

mân, adj., *evil, sinful.*

mânbealu(o), wes, 1, m., *a sin, great evil.*

mancŷn, es, 1, n., *mankind.*

mândream, es, 1, m., *sinful joy, evil.*

mandri(y)hten, es, 1, m., *a lord, master.*

mânhûs, es, 1, n., *a house of sin.*

ma(o)nig, adj., *many a one, many.* G. manags.

manlîca, an, 4, m., *a human image, an image.*

mânsc(e)aða, an, 4, m., *a wretch, sinner, robber.*

mâre: see micel.

mê: see ic.

meâgollice, adv., *bravely, powerfully.*

mearc, e, 2, f., *a border, mark* (myrce). G. marka.

mearchof, es, 1, n., *a field-house, tent.*

mearcla(o)nd, es, 1, n., *a frontier, boundary land.*

mearcþreat, es, 1, m., *a frontier host, an army.*

mearcweard, es, 1, m., *a frontier guardian, a guardian.*

mear(h)g, es, 1, m., *a horse, steed.*

mece, es, 1, m., *a sword, dagger.*

Mêdas, â, pl., *the Medes.*

medugâl, adj., *merry with wine, joyous.*

meðel, es, 1, n., *a discourse, speech, council.*

meðelstede, es, 1, m., *a place of council, a meeting.*

meld, e, 2, f., *evidence, proof, information.*

meltan, mealt, molten (1), *to melt, dissolve.*

me(æ)n(i)geo, 2, f. (indec.), *a multitude* (menio).

menigu, e, 2, f.,

meoring, e, 2, f., *a danger, obstacle.*

meôwle, an, 4, f., *a maid, virgin.*

mêre, adj.: see mære.

mered eáð, es, 1, m., *a sea-death, death.*

mereflôd, es, 1, n., *a sea-flood, sea.*

merchwearf, es, 1, m., *a sea-shore.*

merestream, es, 1, m., *a sea-stream, sea.*

meretor(r), es, 1, m., *a sea-tower.*

mersc, es, 1, m., *a marsh, fen.*

metan, mæt, meten (1), *to mete, measure.*

mêteþegn, es, 1, m., *a meat-thane, servant.*

metian, ôde, od (6), *to mete, appoint.*

metod, es, 1, m., *a measurer* (of destiny), *God.*

mi(y)cel, adv., *much.*

mid, prep., *with, among.* G. miþ.

mid(d), adj., *mid, middle.*

middangeard, es, 1, m., *the middle earth, earth.*

miht, e, 2, f., *might, power.* In pl., *miracles.*

mihtig, adj., *able, mighty.*

mihtmôd, es, 1, n., *a violent mind, spirit*.

mild, adj., *mild, gentle*. G. milds.

milpaử (pæử), es, 1, m., *a mile path, course*.

milts, e, 2, f., *pity, mercy*.

mîn, adj. pro., *mine*.

mînsian, ôde, od (6), *to lessen, destroy*.

mi(y)rc, es, 1, n., *darkness, a dungeon*.

Misa(h)êl, m., *Mishael*.

mismicel, adj., *less great, smaller, fewer*.

missere, es, 1, n., *a half-year, season*.

môd, es, 1, n., *mind, force*.

môdgeþanc, es, 1, m., n., *mind, thought*.

môdgian, ôde, od (6), *to move boldly, rage*.

môdhæp, adj., *brave, fortunate*.

môdhéâp, es, 1, m., *a brave host*.

môdhwa(e)t, adj., *zealous, courageous*.

môdig, adj., *bold, brave*.

môdor, or, 1 (irreg.), f., *mother*.

môdwæg, es, 1, m., *a proud wave*.

molde, an, 4, f., *dust, earth, ground*.

môna, an, 4, m., *the moon*.

môr, es, 1, m., *a moor, heath, mountain*.

morổon, es, 1, m., *murder, death*.

morgen, es, 1, m., *the morning, morrow*. G. maurgins.

môrheald, adj., *heathy, marshy*.

môtan, môste (irreg.), *must, ought*.

Moyses, es, m., *Moses*.

mûổhael, es, 1, m., *a mouth-omen, wise speech*.

murnan, mearn, mornen (1), *to mourn, lament*.

my(i)cel, mâ(mâ)ra, mæst, adj., *much, many*.

myceles, adv., *much*.

mynd(g)ian, ôde, od (6), *to advise, remind*.

myrce : see mearc.

N.

nâ, adv., *not*.

Naboc(h)odonossor, m., *Nebuchadnezzar*.

nac(o)ud, adj., *naked, bare*.

nægan, de, ed (6), *to address, approach*.

næron = ne wæron, *were not*.

næs = ne wæs, *was not*.

nâgan, nahte (irreg.) (ne, âgan), *to lack, not to have*.

na(l)les (ne, eal(l)), adv., *not at all, not*.

nama, an, 4, m., *a name*.

ne, adv., *not*; conj., *nor*.

neâ(y)dan, de, ed (6), *to force, urge*.

ne(â)h, adv., adj., prep., *nigh* (nŷra, nŷst (neâr, nêhst)).

neaht : see niht.

neâr, adv., adj. : see neâh.

nearwe, adv., *closely, narrowly*.

neât, es, 1, n., *a beast, cattle*.

nemnan, de, ed (6), *to name, call*.

neôd : see nŷd. G. nauþs.

neôsan, ôde, od (6), *to visit, see, explore*.

neôwl, adj., *low, deep*.

nep, es, 1, n., *a neap-tide*.

nerc, es, 1, m., *a refuge*.

nergend, es, 1, m., *a preserver, Lord*.

neri(g)an, ede, ed (6), *to save, preserve*.

net(t), es, 1, n., *a net, canopy*. G. nati.

níð, adj., *dire, intense.*

níð, es, 1, m., *a man, a mortal.*

níð, es, 1, m., *hate, envy.*

níðer (nyðōr), adv., *below.*

níðgeþafa, an, 4, m., *a victim, sufferer.*

níðhete, es, 1, m., *envy, dire hate.*

níðwracu, e, 2, f., *dire exile, punishment.*

nied : see nŷd.

nigoða, num. adj., *ninth.*

niht, e (es), 2, f., *night.* G. nahts.

niht-lang, adj., *night-long.*

nihtscu(w)a, an, 4, m., *nightshade, gloom.*

nihtweard, es, 1, m., *a night-guard.*

nis = ne is, *is not.*

niwe, adj., *new, young.* G. niujis.

no (ne, ð), adv., *not.* G. ni.

Noe, es, m., *Noah.*

norðan, adv., *from the north.*

norðweg, es, 1, m., *a north way.*

nu, adv., *now.* G. nu.

nŷd, e, 2, f., *need, necessity, force* (neðd).

nŷdboda, an, 4, m., *an involuntary messenger.*

nŷde, adv., *necessarily.*

nŷdfara, an, 4, m., *a fugitive, exile.*

nŷdgenga, an, 4, m., *a forced wanderer, exile.*

nyllan = ne willan, nolde (irreg.), *to be unwilling.*

nymðe (nemðe), conj., *except, unless.*

O.

ð, adv., *anywhere, everywhere.*

ðð, adv., *until.*

oððe, conj., *or.*

oðer, num. adj., *another, second.* G. anþar.

ððfæstan, te, ed (6), *to fasten, to fasten upon.*

ððfaran, fōr, faren (4), *to go over, pass through.*

ððlædan, de, ed (6), *to lead out, save, deliver.*

ððstandan, stōd, standen (4), *to perplex, hinder, stay.*

oðþæt, adv., *until that.*

ððþicgan, þeah, þigen (1), *to withdraw.*

ððþringan, þrang, þrungen (1), *to press, force, force away.*

of, prep., *of, from.*

of(e)n, es, 1, m., *an oven, a furnace.* G. auhns.

ofer, prep., *over, above.*

oferbræddan, de, ed (6), *to cover, overspread.*

ofercliman, clam(b), clum(b)en (1), *to overcome, oppress.*

ofercuman, com, cumen (1), *to conquer, overcome.*

oferfæðm(i)an, de, ed (6), *to encompass, spread over.*

oferfaran, fōr, faren (4), *to go over, pass through, overcome.*

ofergangan, gengde (6), irreg., *to go beyond, overcome.*

oferhogian (hycgan), ōde, od (6), *to despise, contemn.*

oferholt, es, 1, n., *a shield.*

oferhy(g)d, es, 1, m., *pride, high-mindedness.*

oferlíðan, láð, liden (2), *to sail over, navigate.*

ofermêdla, an, 4, m., *pride, over-measure.*

oferteldan, teald, tolden (1), *to cover, to throw a tent over.*

ōf(e)st, e, 2, f., *haste, speed;* es, 1, m., n., *the quickest.*

ōfstum, adv., *rapidly, forthwith.*

oft, adv., *oft, often*. G. ufta.

Oht, e, 2, f., *fear, persecution*.

Oht-nied, e, 2, f., *tribulation*.

on, prep., *on, upon, in*.

onbrinnan, bran, brunnen (1), *to fire, kindle*.

onbûgan, beah, bogen (3), *to invade, overwhelm*.

onbyrnan, barn, burnen (1), *to kindle, inflame*.

oncweðan, cwæð, cweden (1), *to say, speak, declare*.

oncyrnan, de, ed (6), *to turn, turn back*.

ondrædan, drêd, dreden (5), *to fear, dread*.

onêgan, de (6), *to fear*.

onettan, te (6), *to hasten*.

onfindan, fand, funden (1), *to find, discover*.

onfôn, fêng, fangen (5), *to receive, contain*.

ongean, prep., adv., *against, again*.

onginnan, gan, gunnen (1), *to begin*.

ongitan, geat, giten (1), *to know, perceive*.

onhætan, te, ed (6), *to heat, kindle*.

onhicgan, hogode, od (6), *to reflect, consider*.

onhnigan, hnâh, hnigen (2), *to bow, worship*.

onhrêran, de, ed (6), *to move, rouse*.

onhw(y)eorfan, hwearf, hworfen (1), *to turn, change*.

onlang, adj., *long, continual*.

onlîhan, lâh, ligen (2), *to grant, bestow*.

onlîhtan, te (6), *to enlighten*.

onlûcan, leac, locen (3), *to unlock, loosen*.

onmældan, de, ed (6), *to announce, inform*.

onriht, adj., *just, true*.

onsâcan, sôc, sacen (4), *to refuse, deny*.

onsælan, de, ed (6), *to unbind*.

onseôn, seah, sewen (1), *to see, to look upon*.

onslûpan, sleap, slopen (3), *to glide on*.

onstellan, stealde, steald (6), *to appoint, establish*.

onswellan, swæl, swol(l)en (1), *to swell*. O. E. sweal.

ontreôwan, de, ed (6), *to trust, confide in*.

onþeôn, þeah, þogen (3), *to engage, undertake*.

onwacan, wôc, wacen (4), *to awake, arise*.

onwist, e, 2, f., *a station, abode*.

open, adj., *open*.

or, es, 1, n., *a beginning, van (of an army)*.

ord, es, 1, m., *a beginning, author*.

ordfruma, an, 4, m., *a chief, head, author*.

orðancum, adv., *skilfully*.

orettan, te (6), *to contend for, to fight*.

orla(e)g, es, 1, n., *death, fate*.

orlege, es, 1, m., *war, strife*.

orlege, adj., *fatal, hostile*.

ortrŷwe (treôwe), adj., *distrustful, despondent*.

orwên, adj., *hopeless*. M. 253.

ôtor, adv., *over, beyond, beside*.

ôwiht, e, 2, f., *naught*.

P.

pað (pæð), es, 1, m., *a path*.

Pers(e)as, a (pl.), *the Persians*.

R.

ræd, es, 1, m., *counsel, opinion, advantage.*

rædan, de, ed (6), *to read, rule, interpret.*

rædfæst, adj., *firm in counsel, steadfast.*

rædléás, adj., *rash, headstrong.*

ræran, de, ed (6), *to rear, raise.*

ræs, es, 1, m., *a rush, course.*

ræst, e, 2, f., *rest, sleep* (no pl.).

ræswa, an, 4, m., *a chief, leader.*

rand, es, 1, m., *a border, shield.*

randburh, ge, 2, f. (irreg.), *a shield-wall, a defence.*

randgebeorh(g), es, 1, m., *a protecting shield.*

randwiga, an, 4, m., *a shielded warrior, a warrior.*

randwiggend, es, 1, m., *a shield-bearer, warrior.*

réad (réod), adj., *red.* G. rauds.

reaf, es, 1, n., *clothing, spoil.*

récan, rohte, geroht (6), *to care, reck.*

reccan, re(a)hte, gere(a)ht (6), *to recount, relate.*

re(c)can, ræc, recen (1), *to rule.*

reccend, part. adj., *ruling.*

reced, es, 1, n., *a house, temple, palace.*

réðe, adv., *cruelly, evilly;* adj., *cruel, fierce.*

réðemód (hréðe), adj., *fierce-minded, fierce.*

reg(e)n, es, 1, m., *rain, a storm.*

regnþéof, es, 1, m., *a great spoiler, thief; regn* is a frequent prefix.

réofan, réaf, rofen (3), *to deprive, break.*

reord, e, 2, f., *speech, food, a word.*

reordberend, es, 1, m., *speech (food)-bearing; a prince, man.*

reordi(g)ean, ôde, od (6), *to harangue, speak.*

rest (ræst), e, 2, f., *rest, sleep, a couch.* G. rasta.

restan, te, ed (6), *to rest, remain.*

ríce, adj., *rich, powerful.*

ríce, es, 1, n., *a kingdom, reign.*

riht, adj., *right, straight.* G. raihts.

riht, es, 1, n., *a law, right.* G. garaihtei.

rím, es, 1, m., *a count, number.*

rincgetæl, e, 2, f., *a martial number, host.*

rodo(e)r, es, 1, m., *the firmament.*

rodorbeorht, adj., *heavenly-bright, clear.*

róf, adj., *famous, renowned.*

Ruben, es, m., *Reuben.*

rûm(e), adj., *broad, wide.* G. rums.

rûme, adv., *broadly, widely.*

rûn, e, 2, f., *a mystery, letter.* G. runa.

rûncræftig, adj., *skilled in mystery, wise.*

rÿman, de (6), *to enlarge, make room.*

ryne, es, 1, m., *a course, race.* G. runs.

S.

sae, es, 1, m., f. (irreg.), *a sea.* M. 100.

sæbearg, es, 1, m., *a sea-mountain, sea.*

sæci(y)r, es, 1, m., *ebb of the sea, a turning.*

sæd, es, 1, n., f., *seed, sowing.* G. seds.

sæfæsten, es, 1, n., *a sea-fastness, bulwark.*

sæ-faroð, es, 1, m., *a sea-wave, wave.*

sægrund, es, 1, m., *the sea-ground, depth.*

sæl, es, 1, m., e, 2, f., *fortune, opportunity.*

sælâf, c, 2, f., *the spoil of the sea.*

sæld (sealt), adj., *salt.*

sæleoda (lîda), an, 4, m., *a seaman, sailor.*

sæman, es, 1, m., *a seaman.*

sæstrêam, es, 1, m., *sea, ocean.*

sæwæg, es, 1, m., *a sea-way, sea.*

sæ-waroð, es, 1, m., *a sea-shore, shore.*

sæweall, es, 1, m., *a sea-wall, rampart.*

sæwicing, es, 1, m., *a sea-dweller, pirate, viking.*

Salem, f., *Salem.*

Salomon, es, m., *Solomon.*

samnian, ôde, od (6), *to collect, assemble.*

sang(c), es, 1, m., *a song* (song). G. saggws.

sand, es, 1, n., *sand, earth, shore.*

sâwl, e, 2, f., *soul, life* (sawol). G. suiwala.

scacan, scêoc, scacen (5), *to shake, stir.*

sceado(w), e, 2, f., (w)es, 1, m., *a shadow, shade.*

sceaðan, sc(e)ôd, sceaðen (4), *to injure, scathe.*

sceaft, es, 1, m., *a shaft, spear.*

scealc, es, 1, m., *a servant, soldier.*

scêat, es, 1, m., *a shore, region.*

sceôn, ôde (scŷde) (6), *to fall to, to happen.*

sceôtend, es, 1, m., *a shooter, archer.*

sci(y)ld, e, 2, f., *a debt, sin.*

scildan, de, ed (6), *to shield, protect.*

scildhreoða, an, 4, m., *a shield, buckler.*

scîma, an, 4, m., *shining, a glimmer.*

scînan, sc(e)ân, scinen (2), *to shine, gleam.*

scip, es, 1, n., *a ship.* G. skip.

sci(y)ppend, es, 1, m., *a creator, God.*

scîr, adj., *bright, clear* (Eng. sheer). G. skeirs.

scræf, es, 1, n., *a den, cave.*

scrîðan, scrâð, scrið(d)en (2), *to go, wander, penetrate.*

scûfan, scêâf, scofen (3), *to shove forth, push away.*

scûr, es, 1, m., *a shower, storm.* G. skura.

scyld, es, 1, m., *a shield.*

scyllan (sculan), sc(e)olde, (irreg.), *shall, to be obliged.*

scyrian, ede, ed (6), *to divide, allot.*

se (seô, þæt), ast, pro., *the, he, who;* seþe, *he who.*

scalt, adj., *salt.* G. salt.

searo-(w)es, 1, n., *equipment, weapons.*

sêcan, sôhte, gesoht (6), *to seek, search.*

secgan, sægde (saêde), gesægd (6), *to say, tell.*

sefa, an, 4, m., *mind.*

segel, es, 1, m., n., *a sail.*

segen, es, 1, m., n., *a sign, standard.*

seglrôd, e, 2, f., *a sail-cross.*

segne, e, 2, f., *a net.*

sêl, ra(la), est, adj., *good, happy.*

seld (seald), es, 1, n., *a tent, throne, palace.*

seledrcam, es, 1, m., *hall-joy, joy.*

sellîc, adj., *strange, worthy* (syllîc).

sendan, de, ed (6), *to send, send forth.* G. sandjau.

Sennar, e, f., *Shinar.*

Sennare, a, pl., *people of Shinar.*

seofon, num. adj., *seven.* G. sibun.

seolfer, es, 1, n., *silver.* G. silubr.

seomian, Óde, od (6), *to oppress, harass.*

Seon, es, m., *Sion.*

setlrâd, e, 2, f., *a setting* (of the sun).

settend, es, 1, m., *a disposer.*

sew(i)an, te (6), *to show, teach.*

sibgedriht, e, 2, f., *a kindred host.*

sibgemæg, es, 1, m., *a kinsman.*

sîd, adj., *vast, broad.*

sîð, re, est, adj., *late.*

sîð, Or, Ost, adv., *late* (sup., âst, est, mest).

sîð, es, 1, m., *a journey, lot, time, occasion.*

sîðboda, an, 4, m., *a herald, messenger.*

sîððan, adv., prep., *after, then, since, after that.*

sîðfæt, es, 1, m., n., *a course, journey.*

sîðian, Óde, od (6), *to journey, proceed.*

si(y)(e)ndon : see wesan.

sige, es, 1, m., *victory.*

sigebŷme, an, 4, f., *a trump of triumph.*

sigecyning, es, 1, m., *a king of victory, a victor.*

Sigelware(as), â, m. pl., *the Ethiopians.*

sigerîce, es, 1, n., *a conquered realm.*

sigerîce, adj., *rich in victory.*

sigetiber, es, 1, n., *a sacrifice of triumph.*

sigor, es, 1, m., *victory.*

sigorweorc, es, 1, n., *a work of victory, triumph.*

Simeon, es, m., *Simeon.*

sîn, pos. adj., *his.*

sinc, es, 1, n., *treasure, silver.*

sinc(e)ald, adj., *very cold, ever cold.*

singan, sang, sungen (1), *to sing.*

Sion, c, f., *Sion.*

sittan, sæt, seten (1), *to sit.*

slæp, es, 1, m., *sleep.* G. sleps.

slean, slôh(g), slægen (4), *to strike, slay, cast.*

slûpan, sleâp, slopen (3), *to glide, slip.*

snâw, es, 1, m., *snow.* G. snaiws.

snell, adj., *quick.*

snelle, adv., *quickly.*

sno(t)tor, adj., *wise, skilful, prudent.*

snyttro, 2, f. (indec.), *skill, sagacity.*

sôð, adj., *true, just.*

sôð, es, 1, n., *truth.* Also used adverbially.

sôðcwide, es, 1, m., *a true saying, utterance.*

sôðfæst, adj., *true, faithful.*

sôðwundor, es, 1, n., *a true wonder, great wonder.*

somni(ge)an, Óde, od (6), *to gather, assemble.*

somo(u)d, adv., *together.*

sona, adv., *soon.* G. suns.

sorh(g), es, 1, n., e, 2, f., *care, sorrow.*

spannan, spên, spannen (5), *to span, draw.*

spêd, e, 2, f., *speed, success.*

spel, es, 1, n., *a word, message.* G. waurd. •

spelboda, an, 4, m., *a herald, messenger.*

spe(l)lian, Óde, od (6), *to speak, act for another.*

spildsîð, es, 1, m., *a dangerous journey.*

spillan, de, ed (6), *to spoil, de-stroy.*

spiwan, spåw, spiwen (2), *to spew, foam, reject.*

spor, es, 1, n., *a trace, track.*

spowan, speów, spowen (5), *to thrive, prosper.*

spræc, e, 2, f., *speech, discourse.*

sprecan, spræc, sprecen (1), *to speak, say.*

staðol, es, 1, m., *a place, station.*

stæð, es, 1, n., *a shore, bank.*

stæfn : see stefn.

stån, es, 1, m., *a stone, rock.* G. stains.

standan, stód, standen (4), *to stand.*

starian, óde, od (6), *to gaze, stare.*

steáp, adj., *steep.*

stefen, e, 2, f., *a voice, sound, message.*

steorra, an, 4, m., *a star.*

stêpen, te, ed (6), *to exhalt, dignify.*

stigan, ståh, stigen (2), *to rise, ascend, advance.*

stille, adj., adv., *still, quietly.*

storm, es, 1, m., *a storm, tempest.*

stræt, e, 2, f., *a street, road, course.*

streám, es, 1, m., *a stream, river.*

strúdan, streád, stroden (3), *to despoil, destroy.*

styran, de (6), *to hold, restrain.*

styrian, ede, ed (6), *to stir, move.*

súða, an, 4, m., *the south.*

súðan, adv., *from the south.*

súðweg, es, 1, m., *a south way, southerly.*

súðwind, es, 1, m., *the south wind.*

sum, adj. pro., *some, a certain one.* G. sums. Also a suffix.

sumo(e)r, es, 1, m. (irreg.), *summer.*

sund, es, 1, m., n., *a sea, sound.*

sundor, adv., *apart, separately.*

sundorgifu, e, 2, f., *a special gift, endowment.*

sunne, an, 4, f., u, e, 2, f., *the sun.* G. sunna(o).

sunu, å, 3, m., *a son.* G. sunus.

súsl, es, 1, n., *sulphur, torment.*

swå, adv., *so, thus.*

swapan, sweóp, swapen (5), *to sweep* (away).

swæs, adj., *sweet, dear.*

swefan, swæf, swefen (1), *to sleep, fall asleep.*

swefen, es, 1, n., *a dream.*

swefnian, ede, ed (6), *to dream.*

sweg, es, 1, m., *a sound, heat* (crackling of fire).

sweltan, swealt, swolten (1), *to die, perish* (swelter).

sweord, es, 1, n., *a sword.*

sweordwigend, es, 1, m., *a sword-wielder, warrior.*

sweót, es, 1, m., *a band, crowd.*

swerian (swór), ede, sworen (4), (6), *to swear, affirm on oath.*

swið, rå, óst, adj., *strong,*

swiðe, adv., *eagerly, strongly.*

swiðmód, adj., *strong-minded, arrogant.*

swiðrian, óde, od (6), *to grow strong, prevail.*

swigian, óde, od (6), *to be silent, cease.*

swi(y)lc, adj. pro., *such, such as.*

swi(y)lce, adv., *such that, so.*

swipian, óde, od (6), *to shake.*

swor (går), adj., *sore.*

swutol, adj., *clear, manifest.*

sylf (self, seolf), adj., *same, self-same.* Used with pronouns in same case and gender.

sy(e)llan, sealde, seald (6), *to sell, give.*

symb(e)l, es, 1, n., *a meal, feast.*

syn(n), e, 2, f., *sin.*

synfull, adj., *sinful.*

T.

tâc(e)n, es, 1, n., *a sign, token.*
G. taikns.

tæcan, hte, ht (6), *to show, teach.*

tân, es, 1, m., *a twig, shoot.*

telga, an, 4, m., *a branch, bough.*

tempel, es, 1, n., *a temple.*

teohian (teón), ôde, od (6), *to decree, appoint.*

teónful, adj., *malignant, reproachful.*

teón-hête, es, 1, m., *dire hate.*

teso (teosu), e, 2, f., *affliction, destruction.*

tîd, e, 2, f., *time, tide, season.*

tî(ÿ)r, es, 1, m., *glory, splendor.*

tîr-eádig, adj., *greatly blessed, renowned.*

tîr-fæst, adj., *very firm, glorious.*

tô, prep., *to, for.*

tôdrîfan, drâf, drifen (2), *to scatter, drive asunder.*

tôdwæscan, de, ed (6), *to suppress, extinguish.*

tôhweorfan, hwearf, hworfen (1), *to scatter, depart.*

torht, adj., *clear, bright.*

tôsomne, adv., *together.*

tôscûfan, sceáf, scufen (3), *to separate, scatter.*

tôswapan, sweóp, swapen (5), *to sweep, cast away.*

tôswendan, de, ed (6), *to dash aside, shake off.*

tôwrecan, wræc, wrecen (1), *to banish, exile.*

tredan, træd, treden (1), *to tread, pass over.*

treddian, ôde, od (6), *to step, tread.*

treów, es, 1, n., *a tree.* G. triu.

treów, e, 2, f., *faith, trust.*

treówe, an, 4, f., *a covenant, promise.*

trum, adj., *firm, strong.*

trymian, ede, ed (6), *to prepare, strengthen.*

tuddor-teónde, adj., *producing offspring.*

tungel, es, 1, n., *a star, planet.*

twâ, num. adj., *two.* G. twai.

twelf, num. adj., *twelve.* G. twalif.

tweón, adj., *between* (betweón).

twig, es, 1, n., *a twig, branch.*

tÿn-hund, es, 1, n., *ten hundred.* M. 142.

TH.

þâ, adv., *then* (þa . . . þa, *then . . . when*).

þær, adv., *there* (þær . . . þær, *there . . . where*).

þæs, adv., *thus, whereby* (þæs þe, *because that*).

þæt: see se.

þæt, conj., *that, so that.* G. þata.

þætte, conj., *that, so that.*

þafi(g)an, ôde, od (6), *to allow, obey.*

þanc, es, 1, m., *thanks, favor.*

þancian, ôde, od (6), *to thank.*

þe, art. (indec.), *the, who.* Used in all cases.

þê(a)h, adv., conj., *yet, though, however.* G. þauh.

þeáw, es, 1, m., *a habit.* In pl., *morals.*

þeccan, þeahte, geþeaht (6), *to cover, conceal.*

þeg(e)n, es, 1, m., *a thane, servant.*

þegu, e, 2, f., *service.*

þenden, adv., *while.*

þengel, es, 1, m., *a king, prince.*

þeód, e, 2, f., *people, nation* (þeódan).

þeód(e)n, es, 1, m., *a prince, lord.*

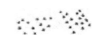

þeóden-hold, adj., *loyal, faithful to God.*

þeódmægen, es, 1, n., *the power of the people, a great power.*

þeódscîpe, es, 1, m., *people, law of the nation.*

þeo-nŷd (þeów-nêd), e, 2, f., *servitude, penal suffering.*

þeóstru, e, 2, f., *darkness;* (þeostor, indec.).

þes, dem. pro., *this.*

þi(y)der, adv., *thither.*

þîn, pos. pro., *thine.* G. þeins.

þincan, þuhte (irreg.), *to seem, appear.* Used impersonally (*methinks*).

þing(i)an, ôde, od (6), *to speak, pray, intercede.*

þolian, ôde, od (6), *to suffer, endure.*

þon, adv., *then.*

þonne, adv., *then;* (þonne . . . þonne, *then* . . . *when*).

þon(ne), conj., *than.*

þracu, e, 2, f., *force, boldness.*

þræcwîg, es, 1, m., *a bold fight, battle.*

þrag(h), e, 2, f., *a time, space.*

þreá(g), eá, m., f., n., *suffering, calamity.*

þreánîed (nŷd), e, 2, f., *penal suffering, torment.*

þreó(ŷ), num. adj., *three.* G. þreis.

þridda, num. adj., *third.*

þrowi(g)ean, ôde, od (6), *to suffer, endure.*

þryŷ, e, 2, f., *strength, a multitude.*

þrŷmfæst, adj., *bold, majestic.*

þrŷmlîce, adv., *boldly, bravely.*

þrŷm(m), es, 1, m., *power, greatness.*

þrysmian, ôde (ede), od (6), *to annoy, disquiet.*

þrŷ(î)st, adj., *bold, daring.*

þûfe, es, 1, m., *a branch, standard.*

þunian (þunerian), ede, ed (6), *to thunder, resound.*

þurh, prep., *through.*

þurfan, þorfte (irreg.), *to need.*

þurstig, adj., *thirsty.*

þurhglêdan, de, ed (6), *to heat through.*

þurhwadan, wôd, waden (4), *to penetrate, pass through.*

þûsendmæl, e, 2, f., *a division by thousands.*

þûsendmælum, adv., *by thousands.*

þŷ : see se.

þŷlæs, conj., *lest that.*

U.

ufan, adv., prep., *above, from above.*

uhttîd, e, 2, f., *before dawn.*

unblîŷ(e), adj., *sad, joyless;* adv., *sadly.*

unceapunga, adv., *freely, without price.*

uncûŷ, adj., *unknown* (uncouth).

under, prep., *under, beneath.* G. undar.

unforbærned, part. adj., *unburned, unhurt.*

unforht, adj., *fearless.*

ungelîc, adj., *unlike.*

ungescéad, adv., *vastly, hugely;* adj., *vast.*

ungrund, adj., *vast, boundless.*

unhleów, adj., *unsheltering.*

unhold, adj., *unkind, untrue.*

unlytel, adj., *great.*

unræd, es, 1, m., *evil counsel, unwisdom.*

unriht, es, 1, n., *wrong, injustice.*

uhritdôm, es, 1, m., *wrong, unrighteousness.*

unrîm, es, 1, m., unrîma, an, 4, m., *a countless number.*

unscynd, adj., *unstained, honorable.*

unswîclend, adj., *unfailing, unceasing.*

unwâclice, adv., *boldly, strongly.*

unweaxen, adj., *young, ungrown.*

up, prep., *up, on.*

upcyme, es, 1, m., *source, rising.*

uplang, adj., *erect.*

uppe, adv., *above.*

up-ridan, râd, riden (2), *to ride up, aloft.*

uprodor (er), es, 1, m., *the firmament, heaven.*

ûser (ûre), pos. pro., *our.* G. unsar.

ûsic : see ic.

ût, adv., *out.*

ûtan, adv., prep., *about, around,* (ymbûtan, *round about*).

V (W).

wadan, wôd, waden (wæden) (4), *to wade, to go through.*

waðema, an, 4, m., *a wave-stream, ware.*

waðian, ede, ed (6), *to drive.*

wa{ð}(u), e, 2, f., *a way, a course.* G. wigs.

wæc(c)lan, ôde, od (6), *to watch.*

waêd, e, 2, f. (waêde, es, 1, n.), *clothing, a garment.*

wæfer, adj., *changing, surrounding.*

wæg, es, 1, m., *a wave.*

wægfaru, e, 2, f., *a wave-road, sea.*

wægstrêam, es, 1, m., *a wave-stream, wave.*

wælben, ne, 2, f., *a battle-wound, corpse.*

wælcêasega, an, 4, m., *a slaughter-chooser, raven.*

wælfæ{ð}m, es, 1, m., *embrace of death, fatal grasp.*

wælgryre, es, 1, m., *battle-terror, deadly horror.*

wælhlence, an, 4, f., *a slaughter-chain, armor.*

wælhrêow, adj., *fierce, bloodthirsty.*

wælmist, es, 1, m., *slaughter-mist, smoke of battle.*

wælnett, es, 1, n., *a fatal net, battle-net.*

wælni{ð}, es, 1, n., *cruelty, fatal hate.*

wælsliht, e, 2, f., *slaughter, great slaughter.*

wæp(e)n, es, 1, n., *a weapon.*

wæpned-cyn, es, 1, n., *a weapon-bearer, man, male.*

wær, e, 2, f. (wære, an, 4, f.), *a compact, covenant.*

wærfæst, adj., *faithful, covenant-keeping.*

wærgengu, an, 4, m., *a wanderer.*

wæstm, es, 1, m., f., n., *fruit-growth, result.*

wæter, es, 1, n., *water.* G. wato.

wæterscipe, es, 1, m., *a body of water, sea.*

wæterspring (sprync), es, 1, m., *a water-spring, spring.*

wafian, ede, ed (6), *to see, to be amazed.*

wah(g), es, 1, m., *a wall.*

waldend, es, 1, m., *a ruler, lord, the Lord.*

wandian, ôde, od (6), *to fear, to be amazed.*

wêa, an, 4, m., *woe.*

wea, adj., *woeful, desolate.*

wealdan, wêold, wealden (5), *to rule, govern.*

wealhstôd, es, 1, m., *an interpreter, translator.*

weall, es, 1, m., *a wall, rampart.*

weal(l)fæsten, es, 1, n., *a rampart.*

weallan, weôl(l), weallen (5), *to well, gush up.*

wean, es, 1, m., *ruin, misery.*

weard, es, 1, m., *a guard, guardian.*

weardian, ôde, od (6), *to guard, protect.*

wearmlîc, adj., *warm.*

weccan, hte, ht (6), *to arouse, bring forth* (wecgan).

wêdan, de (6), *to rage, rave.*

weder, es, 1, n., *weather, storm.*

wederwolcen, es, 1, n., *a heavy cloud, storm.*

weg, es, 1, m., *a way* (on-weg, *away*).

wegan, wæg, wegen (1), *to bear, move.*

wela, an, 4, m., *weal, prosperity* (pl., *riches*).

wen, ne, 2, f. (wêna, an, 4, m.), *hope, expectation.*

wênan, de, ed (6), *to hope, ween.*

wendan, de, ed (6), *to change, wend, interpret.*

w(e)oh-ges (wih), 1, m., *a turning, error, idol.*

weorc, es, 1, n., *work, grief.* G. waurki.

weorcþeow, es, 1, n. (þeowa, an, 4, m.), *a work-slave, slave.*

weo(u)rðan, wearð, worden (1), *to become, happen.*

weorðmynd, es, 1, n., *honor, dignity.*

weorpan: see wyrpan.

wer, es, 1, m., *a man, husband.*

werbeam, es, 1, n., *race of man, man, warrior.*

werî(ge)an, ôde, od (6), *to guard, hinder, wear.*

werian, ede, ed (6), *to curse.*

wêrîg, adj., *weary, depressed.*

werig, adj., *wicked, accursed.*

werod (ud, ed), es, 1, n., *a host, multitude.*

werþeod, e, 2, f., *a nation, people.*

wesan(beôn), wæs, gewesen (Irreg.), *to be, exist.*

west, adv., *westward, western.*

wêsten, es, 1, n., *a waste, desert.*

wêstengryre, es, 1, m., *desert-terror, fear.*

wîc, es, 1, n., *a camp, village.* G. weihs.

wîcan, wâc, wîcen (2), *to yield, give way.*

wiccungdôm, es, 1, m., *magic, sorcery.*

wîcian, ôde, od (6), *to abide, dwell.*

wîcsteal, es, 1, m., *a camp, military place.*

wîd, adj., *wide.*

wîde, adv., *widely, on every side.*

wîde-ferhð, adj., *magnanimous;* adv., *perpetually, widely.*

wið, prep., *with, against, near.*

wiðerbreca, an, 4, m., *an enemy, adversary.*

wiðfaran, fôr, faren (4), *to escape.*

wîf, es, 1, n., *a wife, woman.*

wîg, es, 1, m., *war, battle, martial force.*

wîga, an, 4, m., *a soldier, warrior.*

wîgblâc, adj., *war-pale, alarmed.*

wîgbord, es, 1, n., *a war-board, shield.*

wîgend, es, 1, m., *a warrior.*

wîgleôð, es, 1, n., *a war-song.*

wîglîc, adj., *warlike, martial.*

wîgtrôd, e, 2, f., *an expedition, army.*

wih(g)gyld, es, 1, n., *an idol, false god.*

wiht, e, 2, f., *aught, anything.*

wild, adj., *wild, fierce.*

wildde̋r, es, 1, n., *a wild beast, deer.*

willa, an, 4, m., *will, desire.*

wi(y)llan, wolde (irreg.), *to will, wish.*

wilnian, ôde, od (6), *to wish, desire.*

wîn, es, 1, n., *wine.* G. wein.

winburh, (g)e, 2, f., *a beloved city.*

wind, es, 1, m., *the wind.*

windan, wand, wunden (1), *to wind, roll, turn.*

windig, adj., *windy.*

windruncen, adj., *drunk with wine, drunken.*

winele̋as, adj., *friendless, forsaken.*

winnaû, wan(n), wunnen (1), *to war, win.*

winsum, adj., *pleasant, winsome.*

winter, es, 1, m., *winter, a year.*

winterbiter, adj., *very cold, bitter cold.*

wînþege, an, 4, f., *wine-bibbing, drinking.*

wîs, adj., *wise.* G. weis.

wîsa, an, 4, m., *a wise man, guide, leader.*

wisdom, es, 1, m., *wisdom, prudence.*

wîs(i)an, (ô)de, od (6), *to guide, instruct.*

wîslîc, adj., *wise.*

wîslîce, adv., *wisely.*

wist, e, 2, f., *food, repast, plenty.*

witan, wiste (wisse) (irreg.), *to know, understand.* G. witan.

wîte, es, 1, n., *calamity, punishment.*

witega, an, 4, m., *a prophet, soothsayer.*

wîte-rod, e, 2, f., *a rod of punishment.*

witian, ôde, od (6), *to appoint, prescribe.*

witig, adj., *wise.*

wîtigdom, es, 1, m., *wisdom, knowledge.*

wît(i)gian, ôde, od, *to foresee, prophesy.*

witod, adj., *appointed, fated.*

wlanc, adj., *proud, haughty.*

wlanc, e, 2, f. (wlance, es, 1, m.), *pride, conceit* (wlenco, e).

wlite, es, 1, m., n., *appearance, beauty.*

wlite-scŷne, adj., *beautiful in face, beautiful.*

wlitig, adj., *attractive, beauteous.*

wlitigan, ôde, od (6), *to beautify, adorn, manifest.*

wôd, adj., *mad, incensed.*

wolc(e)n, es, 1, n., *a cloud, the welkin.*

wolcenfaru, e, 2, f., *heaven's course, a cloud-way.*

wom, es, 1, m., n., *a spot, stain, sin.*

wôma, an, 4, m., *terror, tumult, crash.*

won(n), adj., *wan, pale.*

wôp, es, 1, m., *weeping, a whoop.*

word, es, 1, n., *a word.*

wordcwyde, es, 1, m., *a word, command.*

wordgle̋aw, adj., *wise, skilful in speech.*

word-riht, es, 1, n., *a just law, oral law.*

worn, es, 1, n., *a number, body.*

woruld (weoruld), e, 2, f., *world.*

woruldcræft, e, 2, f., *worldly craft, skill.*

woruld-dre̋am, es, 1, m., *worldly joy, joy.*

woruldgesceaft, e, 2, f., *a worldly creation, creatures.*

woruldlîf, es, 1, n., *worldly life, life.*

woruldrîce, es, 1, n., *a world-kingdom, world.*

woruldspêd, e, 2, f., *worldly success, prosperity, events.*

wrâð, adj., *wroth, angry.*

wra(e)c, e, 2, f., *exile, evil.*

wræcca, an, 4, m., *an exile, (wretch).*

wræclîc, adj., *strange, wondrous.*

wræcmo(a)n, es, 1, m., *a fugitive, an exile.*

wræst, ra, adj., *gentle, good.*

wrætlîc, adj., *ornamental, wonderful.*

wrecan, wræc, wrecen (1), *to avenge, chastise.*

wrec(ce), adj.; *exiled, wretched.*

wrîtan, wrât, writen (2), *to cut, engrave, write.*

wrôht, e, 2, f., *blame, strife, harm.*

wudu, â, 3, m., es, 1, m., *a wood, wood.*

wudubéam, es, 1, m., *a forest tree, tree.*

wuldor, es, 1, m., n., *glory, honor.*

wuldorcyning, es, 1, m., *king of glory, God.*

wuldorfæst, adj., *glorious.*

wuldorgesteald, es, 1, n., *a heavenly mansion, wealth, glory.*

wuldorhama, an, 4, m., *a covering of glory.*

wulf, es, 1, m., *a wolf.* Used as a prefix.

wulfheort, adj., *cruel, wolf-hearted.*

wunden, adj., *bent, twisted.*

wundor, es, 1, n., *a wonder, surprise.*

wundorlîc, adj., *wondrous, strange.*

wunian, ôde, od (6), *to dwell, continue.*

wurðian (weorðian, wurðigean), ôde, od (6), *to honor, worship.*

wurômynd, e, 2, f., *dignity, honor.*

wyll, es, 1, m. (wylla, an, 4, m., e, an, 4, f.), *a well, spring.*

wylm, es, 1, m., *heat, fire, a boiling.*

wyn(n), e, 2, f., *joy, pleasure.*

wyrc(e)an, worhte, geworht (6), *to work, acquire.*

wyrd, e, 2, f., *fate, decree, destiny.*

wyrm, es, 1, m., *a worm.*

wyrnan, de (6), *to warn, refuse.*

wyrresta: see ƒfel.

wyrpan, te (6), *to cast down, overthrow.*

wyrt, e, 2, f., *a root, herb.*

wyrtruma, an, 4, m., *herb-room, a root.*

Y.

ƒcan, hte, ƒht (6), *to increase.*

ƒð(u), e, 2, f., *a wave, flood.*

ƒðlâf, e, 2, f., *a flood-remnant, survival.*

ƒfel, wyrsa, wyrst (wyrresta), adj., *evil.* G. ubils.

yld, e, 2, f., *age.*

yldo (indec.), *age.*

yldra: see eald, *the elder.*

yldran, ena (pl.), 4, m., *elders, ancestors.*

yldu, e, 2, f., *age* (yldâs, *men*).

ymb, prep., *about, around.*

ymbhweo(y)rft, es, 1, m., *a circuit, world.*

ymbwici(y)ean, ôde, od (6), *to encamp about, to dwell around.*

ypplng, e, 2, f., *an expanse.*

yrfeláf, e, 2, f., *an inheritance, hereditary remnant.*

yrfeweard, es, 1, m., *an heir, guardian.*

yrmð (yrmðo), e, 2, f., *distress, misery.*

yrre, adj., *angry;* adv., *angrily.*

ðwan, de, ed (6), *to reveal, manifest.*

J. S. CUSHING & CO., PRINTERS, 115 HIGH STREET, BOSTON.